PIRATE'S PRIZE

STEPHANIE FLYNN

Small Fish Publishing
USA

First edition
Cover design by Stephanie Flynn
ISBN eBook: 978-1-952372-24-7
ISBN paperback: 978-1-952372-25-4
ISBN hardcover: 978-1-952372-26-1
ISBN large print paperback: 978-1-952372-28-5

Also By Stephanie Flynn

Find my catalog at StephanieFlynn.com

Immortal Protector series

0.5 Vampire's Distraction

1 Vampire's Deception

2 Vampire's Secret

3 Vampire's Promise

3.5 Elf Bound

4 Vampire's Demand

Immortal Protector Side Tales

Deer Holiday

Love Claws

Depths of the Heart

Matchmaker in Time series

0.5 Minutes to Live

1 Seconds to Act
2 Hours to Arrive
3 Days to Hide
4 Years to Savor

Pirates in Time series
1 Pirate's Prize
2 Pirate's Treasure
3 Pirate's Plunder

Time Travel Romance Shorts
Fateful Time
One Crazy Time

If you like your urban fantasy without the romance, too, check out Stephanie Flynn's other name, Marie Flynn!

Special Note

While the events of this novel are fiction, the pirate raid on the Spanish divers recovering the gold from the Plate Fleet Wreck of 1715 was real. To this day, millions of dollars in gold remain below the sea off the coast of Florida.

Chapter 1

AT THIRTY-EIGHT YEARS OLD, Emily Porter had spent years scraping by to squirrel away some savings to change her life. She'd done the app coupons, gig jobs, careful budgeting, and apartment hopping when rents increased. And all this time, she'd never loosened the reins. She'd never 'lived' a little. Growing up in poverty, it was all she knew, and she vowed to never be there again.

When she'd met starry-eyed, ambitious Tyler, she was swept away with his big dreams. He'd convinced her to invest her savings in their new joint business venture. Their relationship was young for such a commitment, but at Emily's age, she didn't want to waste time.

She should've.

All the red flags were there, but her rose-colored glasses shrouded them in plain sight. And still, the business had yet to open. Emily hadn't signed any documents. All the while, Tyler spent much of his day lounging at home in pajamas, "working" from his phone, and Emily's day job hours had been cut. She needed a few bucks back to tide her over until the next payday. Text after text was met with excuses.

So she knocked on his door.

Confrontation was rarely a great idea, but Emily was beyond betrayed; she was furious. Her fist connected with his apartment door, likely angering the neighbors, but they hadn't lost five figures in life savings. A muted shuffling came from the other side of the hollow door. Emily stopped and waited.

The door opened to Tyler's surprised face. His hair was dishevelled, like she'd woken him up, and sweatpants hung low on his hips. A wrinkled T-shirt covered his smooth upper body. "Em? What brings you here?"

Normally, he'd move aside. "Are you going to invite me in?"

Tyler glanced over his shoulder as if Emily hadn't seen the mess before. "Now's not a good time."

Emily leaned in close for privacy's sake. "I need my money back. I've texted you many times."

"I saw," he said, but Emily waited a beat for an excuse that didn't come.

"And?" Emily prompted.

"And what?"

She was done being polite. "Give me my money back."

Tyler rubbed the nape of his neck in a dismissive gesture. "No can do. Sorry."

Finally, she got an answer, but it wasn't the one she wanted. "Excuse me?"

"I don't have it."

"Where is my money, Tyler?"

"It's invested." The casualness of the tone wasn't reassuring.

"This is the first I'm hearing about it. Do you have paperwork for me to sign?" Perhaps she'd been too impatient. Getting a business going did take some time. If

Tyler was following through with his promises, she could scrape together a few more gig jobs.

"Why would I have paperwork for you?"

The fury zipped along her body, tensing her. "Partners need to sign paperwork to make the business official both for the city and the IRS. I know that much, Tyler. Don't patronize me."

"Partners?" Tyler said with a chuckle of disbelief. "Partners have to trust each other."

"I gave you all my money. Isn't that enough proof for you?"

A nearby door opened, and a cranky woman scowled at them before closing it again.

In a lower voice, Emily asked, "Can we finish this inside?"

"That's not the problem," Tyler said, ignoring her request for privacy again. "It's that I don't trust *you*. Every time I needed something, you failed to deliver. I can't go into business with someone who's flakey like that."

Emily couldn't believe what she was hearing. How could he consider her to be unreliable? How was that an excuse for the plans they'd made? "I sacrificed for years to save up that money, and I handed it to you up front...for this partnership. I don't understand why you think I'm flakey at all."

Tyler shook his head, but he hardly met her gaze. It was the same discomfort Emily had seen right before her father left her mother. That same crushing pile of guilt was written all over Tyler, and a rock settled in Emily's gut. Rather than own his choice head on, he was trying to avoid the confrontation, the pain.

"Tyler." Her voice lowered. The anger had already drained. The familiar, scary feeling of abandonment creeped under her skin. "Are you telling me there is no 'business' at all?"

His disinterested gaze swung back to her. "There's no business between us."

Emily had done everything right, everything he'd asked. All she wanted was to be loved and cherished by a partner who was committed to her and respectful. Tyler was slipping through her fingers like melted chocolate, the sweetest thing in her life slowly gliding away, and there was nothing she could do to stop it.

"Then what do you need from me? I want this to succeed. I believe in us." Emily reached out to touch his face, but he pulled back.

"Em, the bottom line is when I need you to do something immediately, I can't trust you to listen. Always questioning and so skeptical. We don't have the proper foundation to succeed. It's simply not there."

Emily dropped her hand. Each sentence was like a hammer's swing on her crumbling heart. Emily exhaled a deep breath. He was breaking up with her. "If that's how you feel, then I want my money back."

Tyler shook his head. "I told you the funds are invested."

Emily didn't see how that was an excuse. Sell the stock? Sell the equipment? "Cut me a check. Post-date it if you have to."

"Sorry, babe. Can't do that either."

She lifted her voice. Apartment walls be damned. "I want my money back now."

"That's not how this works." Tyler looked at the floor and smoothed the mop on his head. Emily finally saw the real man—a coward.

"You refuse to start a business with me, after you promised we would. I gave you my money to invest in said business, but now you won't return it. Am I getting this right?"

Tyler's mouth opened, but Emily held out a hand to stop him. "You're a lying, despicable thief."

For the first time since she'd met him, Tyler was speechless.

"Return my money or I'm taking you to court." Emily turned on her heels and left, marching down the apartment building hallway, head held high but tears on the verge of spilling.

From a partner sharing his big dreams to a cold thief in one conversation. Emily had a feeling the small claims division of the district court had too low of limits. She'd never had a reason to check, and she couldn't afford to retain an attorney.

He might've stolen her money, but he really stole her life.

And now the tears fell.

2

Chapter 2

Emily had managed a last-minute shopping gig on an app and pocketed enough coin to tide her over. But months passed, and after one sharply written letter from an attorney, Tyler still hadn't paid her. Shockingly, Emily didn't have the funds to hire additional services, and unshockingly, Tyler hadn't volunteered to return her money. Men who walked away from the women they loved, leaving them destitute, were absolute scum—unworthy of respect or another second of her time. Tyler joined that growing list alongside her father.

She never thought she would have to make a list in the first place, but she'd keep her eye out next time. No one else was going on that list.

Emily had one thing she was looking forward to—the Tall Ships festival. Since Tyler had no reason to use his ticket anymore and she didn't want to go alone, Emily asked her best friends, Robin Hall and Angela Foxe, to keep her company. Neither of them were fans of the idea, but since the festival would never come around Green Bay, Wisconsin, again, Emily couldn't miss this.

"Any word from Robin yet?" Angela asked from the driver's seat of her car. Emily and Angela worked for the same big-box retail store. Emily was usually assigned to stock shelves or to the supervision of the self-checkouts.

She also volunteered to be on the first responders' team in case of a medical emergency. Angela was a tough chick who ran circles around the men in the warehouse. Unlike Emily, Angela was disgruntled by the boring khakis and the store's branded polo, so when Emily dangled the promise of a cute dress, Angela was in. Emily was grateful for a strong arm to lean on. Angela had survived heartbreak—worse than Emily's—and the woman was tough as nails about it.

After a few pints of ice cream and a haircut.

Emily rode shotgun, her body tingling with excitement and anticipation. The international Tall Ships festival had journeyed up the Great Lakes for a weekend visit. People all around gathered to explore maritime history—including both privateers and pirates. Others, weirdos like Emily, would dress in pirate cosplay, showing their fascination with an antique world only seen in movies and books. She checked her screen, and apparently in her single-track focus today, she'd forgotten to unmute her phone. "Oh, yeah. She says she'll meet us there."

"Think she'll show?" Angela asked.

Robin was reserved. A new police officer to the force, she had something to prove while being careful. Robin Hall had a public image to maintain, but after much more begging, Robin reluctantly agreed, too. "I hope so."

"Me, too," Angela said, navigating the car into the lot of the downtown riverside park. Down the hill, naked masts reached for the sky, their sails furled for safety. The moment the shifter moved into park, Emily sprung from the vehicle.

Since it was the middle of summer, and the Halloween stores weren't open yet, Emily urged her friends to order bagged costumes online to join her in spirit. Emily had spent years handcrafting her outfit of brown leather boots, knee breeches, and a leather jerkin over a white tunic, which hid a tank top with a built-in bra. She wore it to every Halloween party and afterward adjusted it as needed for durability, flexibility, and comfort. Last year's party at the University of Wisconsin Green Bay left her with a splash of beer on her tunic. Angela had said it made her shirt more authentic, but Emily explained pirates at sea didn't drink beer, and she still wanted to wear the tunic she'd sewed. Emily spent far too long carefully cleaning the fabric before the stain set in and ruined all her hard work. To finish out her look, Emily's shoulder-length blonde hair was covered under a red kerchief, leaving only a loose lock on the side of her face. A dress couldn't give her feminine curves, not that she'd wear one, anyway.

Angela climbed out of the car and smoothed her dress. "I don't know," she said with pleasant surprise. "This feels a little sexy." Angela chose a ruffled high-low dress, off-the-shoulder black blouse, and a decorative corset on top—the typical pirate wench outfit. Angela twirled the material. "I could get into this."

"You look amazing. Come here." Emily hooked her arm around Angela's and pulled her close for a selfie. Angela's car was in the background, but it didn't matter. Emily didn't want to forget anything about this day. After a few different angles and faces, Emily pulled her best friend through the parking lot and down to the admissions tent.

The excitement put a spring in her step, and while waiting for the line to shorten, she beamed at the ships docked behind them. Emily had purchased tickets months ago, but to board a ship, she needed the stamp on her hand. She pulled out her phone, opened the email confirmation, and brought up the barcoded ticket that granted her access to the ship and a sail tour. She and Tyler were supposed to have a romantic sail on the bay this afternoon, but instead, Robin and Angela were her plus-ones, and she wouldn't trade their company for anything, certainly not a despicable thief who shall not be named again.

"Thanks. I think I like it. When you told me about this stuff, I was thinking of Captain Jack Sparrow, and drunks with too much rum." Angela wriggled her fingers at a guy walking by, and his eyes raked her curvy body. "But I can see why you like this stuff."

Emily's hobby involved pretending to be something she wasn't, daydreaming of a world that no longer existed. She'd been born and raised in Wisconsin, and she'd always dreamed of taking to the seas and sailing away. But her parents weren't interested, if they could afford it, and after Dad ran off, it wasn't in the cards—not even a commercial cruise based out of Florida. When winter came around each year, Emily spent her time reading research materials with contradicting information. And she'd maintain or add to her outfit. Slowly she'd built her savings to change her life—school, a business, or even a round-the-world cruise.

Frankly, she wanted the cruise, but since it was an irresponsible use of funds, she'd held back. And now that wasn't even an option anymore. So this ride on a historical recreation of a seventeenth century ship was the best she was ever getting, and thinking of how close she was brought tears to her eyes.

"There's a few hot guys here, Em. I bet we can find a sexy captain for you."

The idea should be appealing, someone with the same interest as her, but Emily wasn't done with the long-reaching effects of Tyler's betrayal. "I'm not ready to dive back into the dating pool."

"In that case, let's get drinks."

The line shifted closer. "There's no alcohol served."

After a flash of disappointment, Angela said, "Maybe I was talking about the slushies."

"A slushy sounds great." Emily smiled and glanced longingly over her shoulder, trying to convince herself she was finally here. A light breeze sent gentle waves lapping at the dock, and seagulls drifted in the sky, sleek white and gray against the shining sun.

Emily never wanted to forget this. She had been at the festival for a few minutes already, and she hadn't thought to document this momentous day. She pulled her cell phone out of her pouch and nudged Angela. "Say cheese."

Making sure the ships were in the background, Emily snapped a few goofy-faced pictures and several sweet ones. "Robin better get here soon. I need pics with her too."

"Did she send you an update?" Angela craned her neck through the thickening crowd.

Emily checked her phone. "Nothing yet." She took a step closer and skimmed too. About half the festival attendees were decked out like Emily, and she smiled at the plush parrot stitched to a man's shoulder. A woman strolling by wore envious boots with her hair in long red ringlets, reminding Emily of the famous pirate Anne Bonny. Yep, these were her people.

Finally reaching the booth, Emily flashed her digital ticket. The festival worker squinted at the screen. Oh, no. She could not be denied entrance now. Setting down the phone, Emily said, "I have the paper ones in here." In a hurry, she dug in her pouch tied around her waist, fishing for the folded paper she'd printed ahead of time.

"I can see them well enough. Hold out your hand." The worker reached for the ink pad. Emily and Angela held out the backs of their hands and received a cold, wet stamp each. "Have a good time."

Emily beamed. "We will. Thanks!"

Emily slipped the phone back into her pouch, next to her emergency sewing kit, travel sized bottle of ibuprofen, a few first aid items, and some individually wrapped chocolates as a pick-me-up. She expected the vendor food to be a little out of her budget. Emily had thought of everything, and nothing was going to interrupt this awesome day. They headed down the hill toward the water, but Angela tugged her in the wrong direction. Emily protested. "The ships are that way."

"We have to wait for Robin, so let's go shopping! Look at all those vendors just waiting for money. My treat?"

After toeing the line of homelessness too many times, shopping had never appealed to Emily. But she'd set aside funds in case a fellow enthusiast was selling anything that tickled her inner pirate. And Emily was thrilled to see Angela enjoy herself. For that, she could wait to board the ship just a little longer. "I can cover my own. Don't worry about it."

Rows of yellow tents with folding tables bisected the festival grounds. Angela pulled her past several vendors with wares that didn't interest her. "Who wants to buy a fake sword, anyway?"

"I do prefer real ones," Emily said, half joking. The closest thing to a sword she'd ever wielded was a honking, serrated bread knife. But when she regularly cut herself, she could rock a sewing kit like a beast.

"Maybe I can knock one of these hot guys over the head with one, and you can play Emergency Response Team. He might need CPR. You brought your sewing kit, right?" Angela teased with a wicked grin.

"Never leave home without it, but Robin's going to be here soon. I don't need either of us arrested for assault, no matter how hot the guy is."

"Eh, you're no fun."

Emily chuckled and kept moving at Angela's insistence. In the back corner, slightly away from the other vendors, was a withered old woman, sitting in front of glass display cases. Angela leaned closer and gasped.

"What is it?" Emily asked, gazing back at the dock. She patiently waited to hear the creak of the ancient wood beneath her feet as they glided across the calm bay and wished it was the aquamarine blues of the Caribbean Sea.

"How beautiful! Oh, Em, check these out. They'd go great with almost anything."

Emily leaned in. Necklaces and bracelets hung on clear hooks. They were pretty, and they looked expensive—sparkly colors, shiny metals, and ornate patterns. "You could have one for each outfit."

"Good morning, ladies." The old woman stood from her squeaky chair, her raspy voice not much above a whisper. "See anything you like?"

"Everything is beautiful!" Angela pressed a fit to her chest, enamored.

"I can certainly wrap up everything." The old woman chuckled. "But I sense something in the two of you. Especially you." The woman stared at Emily.

"Me?" Emily asked, now paying attention.

"You'd rather be somewhere else. Somewhere far from here." Her crooked finger tapped her knowing temple. She was a little creepy.

Sure, Emily would love to be in the tropics on a sailing cruise, but that was a dream, and this was reality. Glancing at the tall ships anchored at the dock, there was literally nowhere else on earth she'd rather be. Emily smiled. The slightly strange woman was way off. "Not at all. I've been dreaming of seeing ships like these my entire life, and I can't believe they're here. I never want them to go."

"I suspected some wistful thinking there. I have just the thing for you. Come here." The frail vendor urged them to come around to the side of the tent, and she bent down, crooked fingers unlocking a small wooden chest. Emily smiled at its authentic look—like an ancient treasure chest. Now that was something she'd like to have in her collection.

The woman lifted something sparkly, and in the palm of her hand, she held a pair of necklaces. "These powerful gems have been known to grant your truest desire while protecting you from bad humors, so be careful how you use them."

The necklaces sounded cursed, and now Emily was fascinated. Why buy a purple amethyst when you could have one that was haunted with stories of the past? Emily and Angela each took one. The pretty purple gemstones hung on a copper chain, and the ends of them were dipped in melted copper. Not too flashy, a little rustic, and somewhat antique. She loved it.

"How much?" Emily asked immediately.

"Yeah," Angela added. "I'll take this one too."

"Five dollars each." The old woman smiled again.

Emily hated to take advantage. "Come again?"

Angela said, "We'll take these both, but do you have more? We have a friend we're waiting for. She'd just die for one, too."

The old woman chuckled. "If I sense they need them, your friend will get one as well. Let me bag those for you." She held out her hand, and both Emily and Angela returned them for packaging.

While the woman bent to bag them up, Angela dug in her purse and whispered, "This lady's crazy! Five bucks? Can't even get a sandwich for that."

Emily freed a pair of fives, intent on paying a little more to ease the guilt. "They're worth way more than that."

The old woman stood and refused to accept anything beyond the five she'd asked for. With a shrug, Emily and Angela completed the transaction and accepted small brown paper bags with handles.

"Thanks, lady!" Angela said, waving, and they strolled toward the ships. "I still can't believe something this beautiful was so cheap."

"We offered, and she refused," Emily said. "Come on. The barque is open." This time, Emily dragged Angela to the ship, flashed their hand stamps, and walked up the gangway. Emily grinned like a loon and marveled at each step, memorizing it forever.

"What about Robin?" Angela followed.

Emily rubbed the wood rail with her palm, and giddiness rushed through her. Her cheeks hurt already, but still, she couldn't stop smiling. "She'll be here. I'm just going to absorb this whole ship while I can." There were plaques mounted in different areas of the ship, explaining what happened in the past and what the living conditions were like. A vendor sold T-shirts and mugs in the corner, branded with the ship's name. The boards underfoot shifted with each step. The scent of the bay was so much stronger here, and the gentle movements under the lapping of the water were a relaxing sway. She would never be able to sleep on a ship like this. She wondered how the crew did it. Not because of the motion, but because this was a ship from history. Emily lifted out her phone and started snapping pictures.

"You sound like a sponge." Angela said, scanning the faces climbing aboard. "We should've dragged a few hot guys on this tour."

Emily gazed up at the crow's nest, wondering if she could take a trip up the ratlines for a view.

She'd never come down.

"Ladies, for safety packages are not allowed." A member of the ship's crew, wearing neat and clean ship-branded clothing, appeared out of nowhere. He had a sexy accent. "There's a basket on land to store your belongings." Without waiting for a response, he moved on to the next offender.

"There's your hot guy for the tour," Emily said.

Angela snorted. "I am a sucker for an accent."

Emily too.

Just off the ship was a large crate guarded by the man checking stamps.

"I'm not leaving this behind to get stolen," Angela whispered.

"Me neither. He didn't say we couldn't wear them." Emily shrugged.

"True." Angela and Emily dug their necklaces out of their bags and slipped them over their heads.

In the blink of an eye, something went wrong.

Very wrong.

Chapter 3

"STOWAWAY!" A BARREL-CHESTED MAN with an English accent pointed at her accusingly. He wasn't wearing the branded polo like the staff member had been. This guy was rough and dirty—very authentic, and a little scary.

Emily's cheeks flushed at the embarrassment of being singled out. She still held the vendor bag in her hand. She sheepishly smiled and waved it. "It's empty. No rules broken here."

"Sweep the hold for others!" he commanded, in character at a level even Emily admired.

Threadbare cosplayers dashed around the deck to obey orders. None of these people looked like fellow tourists—no cameras, no sunglasses, no sandals, no silly Hawaiian shirts or costumes from a bag. No plush parrots sewed to their shoulders. Perhaps these men were the real crew, who'd come from below deck for the sailing tour.

Emily looked down. The color of the wood was different. Scanning the ship's details, the plaques were gone, and underfoot was a galleon. She swore she'd boarded a barque. The vendor selling T-shirts and mugs in the corner was gone.

Had Emily blacked out? She hadn't been drinking. She didn't take anything unusual.

Emily turned. Where was Angela? Did she find someone to take below deck?

Did Emily hit her head, and now she was dreaming? Or in all her excitement to experience the ships of history, a lifelong dream turned reality, did she concoct a believable fantasy? A true hallucination? She'd built up this moment so much, she'd finally snapped. Emily lifted her hand and touched the copper chain holding the amethyst pendant she'd tucked under her tunic. So her mental break began after their trip to the withered old lady.

If Emily was trapped in her head, she was going to damn well enjoy it.

The large pungent man gripped her arm with a squeeze of a constrictor snake preparing its next meal.

The smile fell from her face. Maybe not so much. Why would she include someone like this in her fantasy?

"Nobody swindles a ride on this vessel." His breath was unfortunate—stale and yeasty.

Going with the flow of her unusual choice to include this guy in her fantasy, Emily twisted her arm from his crushing grasp. "I'm not a stowaway! I bought a ticket, and I can prove it. It's right here." Emily ruffled into the leather pouch tied around her waist and produced the backup paper ticket she'd printed at home. She held it out in offering and the wind rustled it. But the meaty man glared at her, refusing to look at it.

In a lightning-quick strike, he backhanded her cheek, sending stings like dozens of rubber bands snapping across her face. Tears involuntarily filled her eyes. The ticket flitted to the deck and blew through the bulwark and into the water.

Emily cupped her cheek, and her mouth popped open. She wasn't one to demand a manager, since she'd dealt with those kinds of complaints at work frequently, but assault was justified. Emily didn't think this guy would hand over his manager's digits, though. Besides, this was a fantasy. Although it was becoming a little too twisted, even for her tastes.

"Hold your disobedient tongue in the presence of one Captain Donald Sinclair." The captain sneered and ran his beady eyes over her. "You'll earn your unlawful boarding. Scrub the deck." While glaring at her with unwarranted hatred, he shouted, "Fergus! Bring the scoundrel a bucket of water and a brush."

"Aye, sir," Fergus answered, a Scottish man by accent and thin as a twig with bushy red hair. He appeared no older than twenty years of age as he dashed below deck.

The captain leaned in close, as if searching her for a hidden truth, and Emily leaned back. "You're not of King George's country. Where are you from?"

The tall ships traveled the world, visiting groups of ports at a time, and right now, they were sailing the Great Lakes, ergo, the USA. But his grip and his slap hurt, even in her fantasy. She needed to be careful, and she wanted to know what year her hallucination brought her to. There were several King Georges throughout history. "Which King George?"

Apparently, that was the wrong answer. The captain bristled, leaning back to spew his next angry accusation. "The one and only! His majesty took over the Crown just over a year ago. Are you illiterate? Where are you from?"

King George the first began his rule in 1714, so a year later put her in the year 1715. A century not known for being kind to women on ships. Emily felt herself shrink down. What would make the captain less suspicious? "An island off the coast of the colonies," she answered with a slight question, hoping to avoid another slap.

The captain's sharp eye zeroed in on her copper chain. Before she could twist away, the captain's meaty hand squeezed her shoulder, holding her in place, and the other tore the necklace from around her throat. He scrutinized his ill-gotten gains, face darkening as he wound up for the next lashing.

Escape. All she could think of was escaping. Emily looked for the gangway, but it was gone. She spun. Nothing but glinting bright blue waters stretched on the horizon. Where were Michigan's shores? Wisconsin's? Her fantasy really filled out the details. Even the air felt...salty. Emily faced the captain again. Unfortunately, too many details.

"Thief! You dare steal from my ship? From the Sea Trading Company?" The captain shook her necklace and growled his words in pure rage. "You know what the punishment is for theft."

Anything she might tell him would end with another slap. Emily shook her head, breath caught in her throat. The captain slipped the purple gem into a pocket in his breeches just as the twiggy redhead returned with the bucket and a brush.

"Sir, as ye requested." Fergus set them down and scurried back to work without delay.

Ignoring Fergus's interruption, the captain said, "The cat. Ever heard of it?"

Emily nodded, so she didn't anger him further. She'd read about the cat-o'-nine-tails, a whip with nine lengths and nine knots at the ends. Was this some form of self-punishment? Was she conjuring this physical pain as punishment for her stupidity in falling for Tyler's thievery? If that was the case, she was over it. She was over Tyler's betrayal, and this whipping was unnecessary.

"Swab this deck clean enough to eat from, while I determine how many lashes I'll be personally delivering." The captain smirked and shoved her bodily to the deck. She landed with a sharp pain to her knee, and the captain hawked a loogie right by her leg.

Gross. Emily's face curled with disgust. The filthy captain, a greedy, selfish brute, strolled away with her necklace, but he had the audacity to accuse her of thievery and punish her with a whipping for it. Emily wasn't waiting around for it. She needed to find Angela and get the hell off this ship...

...or out of her own head.

She hated to go there, but she did—would the whipping wake her out of this twisted version of the history she adored? And if this was her fantasy, she would've included her best friend. So where was Angela? Emily craned her neck but couldn't see her. She couldn't hear her either.

"Angela?" she called carefully, so the captain wouldn't return with more excuses to punish her.

No response from anyone. The crew moved around on deck, attending their duties.

"Angela?"

No laughter, no screams of ecstasy or shrieks of terror. Was she unconscious?

Emily's knee ached, and if the slap on the cheek and the squeeze of the shoulders were indicators, Emily would rather figure out something else than endure a whipping. Emily grimaced at the condition of the deck, stood up, and craned her neck around. Blue-green waters of the Caribbean. Salty air. A small rocky projection was within swimming distance, but that would be a different sort of punishment.

Her fantasy really did the details well.

Some could've been left out.

The twig Fergus rushed up to her and pointed at the deck. In a low voice, he said, "Return tae work right noo. If th'captain sees ye shirking orders, he'll add many more lashes. Trust me when I say ye dinny want them."

"But—"

"Dinny argue. Jus' dae." Fergus set his jaw firmly and glared at her in warning.

Emily folded down on her aching knees. Expecting the redhead to stand by to make sure she followed orders, she lifted the wire brush and dunk it into the water. She started brushing and looked up for approval, but Fergus was gone.

Emily sighed. The deck was covered in bird droppings, smears of blood, and liquids of unknown origin. She stroked the bristles across the wood planks. Overhead, sails flapped as they lost the wind. She shielded her eyes against the sun to watch the meager crew climb the ratlines and adjust the yardarms. Wood groaned its protest. There was no joy in their dirty faces, nor pride in their work, and no downtime. They were machines, not men happy to be at sea.

Emily herself struggled to find the enjoyment she expected to find on a ship. She continued lazily scrubbing, determined to never complain about public toilets again. She worked her way around barrels of whatever goods the ship traded, careful not to get stepped on. Her arm was tired already. She swiped a sweaty forearm across her forehead, wishing for a shower.

Loud boots approached across the hardwood, alerting Emily to the captain's return. A pit formed in her stomach. She exhaled a shaky breath and stood.

Captain Donald Sinclair carried the famous whip in his hand and an unnervingly friendly demeanor. "You'll be pleased to discover I've sentenced you to only ten lashes. The entire crew shall be watching—as a warning to them, as much as to you."

At the terrible news, Emily's eyes darted over the rail. The desolate spit of land was long gone. How else was she going to get out of this? Men were treated worse than dogs on this ship, and a woman would be so much worse, Emily didn't want to imagine it. But if the captain meant to whip her, there were two things the crew was bound to notice.

The captain gripped her forearm—as if she'd planned to escape. "Secure the stowaway for punishment!"

A pair of grimy men captured her arms and pulled her face forward to the mainmast. This was going to happen, and she was out of ideas. Emily struggled against their grip and cried out, "Please don't! I beg of you. I didn't stowaway, and I didn't steal anything. The necklace is mine, I swear!"

The men strapped her wrists, forcing her to hug the mast.

Fergus leaned in close and tugged on the binds. He whispered, "Dinny fight it. Captain won't quit 'til it's done. Th'more ye struggle, th'worse it feels."

Hot tears stung her cheeks while the two men wrenched the biting rope. "Please. Make him stop."

"I canny. Nae one can," he said softly. "But I wish I could."

The men and Fergus left her, and time stretched as Emily awaited the first searing strike. She squeezed her eyelids shut and wished she'd taken a chance swimming with the sharks.

From behind her, the captain said, "This is what befalls any of you for stealing passage or merchandise from the Sea Trading Company. Fergus, cut away the jerkin."

Emily's heart punched up her throat. She sucked in a desperate breath, and yanked and twisted her wrists, rope biting into her flesh. They couldn't find out her secret. This couldn't be happening. When was she going to wake up?

4

Chapter 4

"SAILS!" A VOICE CALLED from above her. Emily craned her neck the best she could. In the crow's nest, a man pointed south. She followed his finger. Sails at a distance were approaching.

"What colors does she fly?" Captain Donald Sinclair responded with an unusual edge to his voice, almost a hint of fear. The captain lifted a spyglass from his pocket and held it to his eye as he surveyed the horizon.

Thrilled for a delay in her unfit punishment, Emily frantically attempted to escape her binds. And then what? She didn't know, but staying here and doing nothing was not in her nature. How did she go from the happiest day of her life to prepared for a whipping that was infamously cruel?

She remembered boarding the barque, certain it was a barque. Then an employee of the Tall Ships organization told her no merchandise was allowed. So, she and Angela had put on their matching necklaces rather than leave them ashore and risk their theft. The irony only frustrated Emily more.

The withered old lady had said, 'These powerful gems have been known to grant your true desire...' Emily had wished for an adventure on the sea since she was young, and here she was, but she didn't care what anyone said—magic wasn't real. The possibility of time travel was ludicrous, scientifically impossible.

But the condition of this galleon and its crew was far too real to be cosplay alone. The soft blue-green waves and gentle salty breeze of tropical air were damned convincing. Had the necklace transported her through time by some mystical means? Then Emily's only way home was to put on the magic necklace again. But how was she going to find it? And where was Angela?

"She's flying the French colors!" the crewman above shouted back.

Captain Sinclair dropped the spyglass and grunted. He collapsed the tool and lowered it to his side.

"Shall we attempt communications, captain?" Fergus asked carefully.

"All hands bring her to!" the captain shouted, and the crew sprang into action, leaving Emily stranded and helpless.

The captain approached and sniveled in her ear, "Expect to receive your punishment after my dealings with the French. Refrain from attempting to escape. There's nowhere for you to go." He chuckled.

A glint of light came from his pocket—her necklace poked out of his breeches. He still had it! If she could free herself and rush him, she could steal it back and put it on before anyone could catch her. It was the best plan she had. It was the only plan.

The captain returned to the rail with the spyglass, keeping tabs on the incoming ship.

Emily worked at the ropes binding her hands while the crew slowed the behemoth ship. She had learned passing ships frequently shared information on the seas, so Captain Sinclair's decision to slow wasn't alarming, and Emily was grateful for the extended reprieve.

"Th'vessel's approaching rapidly." Fergus stood at his shoulder. "She'll be wit'in firing distance soon. Is she a man-o'-war?"

"Barque." The captain's eye flashed, and the color drained from his face. Something was wrong. "Jorgenson!"

A bulky crew member rushed to the captain's side, ready for orders.

"Gather all available hands and hide the provisions in the carpenter's walk."

Jorgenson nodded, and men scurried below deck with fear on their brows. They knew what was happening, but Emily didn't. She could guess it wasn't good. She twisted, pulling at her ropes, trying to stretch the length just enough to slip free.

"To the rest of you, brace round forward, and set the courses. Flank speed immediately!" The captain slipped the spyglass into his pocket and paced the deck, ignoring Emily. The crew adjusted the sails to catch the ocean breeze. Instead of slowing, he was metaphorically running. What caused the sudden change in plans?

Emily's wrists ached as she pulled at the ropes holding her prisoner, and the roughness cut through her skin.

The boom of a cannon echoed across the water, and the shot splashed alarmingly close by—a warning even Emily understood. The captain raised the spyglass to his eye once again. "Belay those orders!" he shouted with a quiver in his voice.

Fergus returned to the captain's side while keeping an eye on the crew's work. "Sir, have the French signaled us?"

Emily strained around the mast. The other ship was close enough to see. The French flag lowered with jerky movements, and a black flag with a skull and crossbones took its place. "You got to be kidding me." For a second, she chuckled at the ludicrousness of it all. Pirates? Actual pirates? The real ones were nothing like the movies. If she thought Captain Donald Sinclair was an animal, pirates were the things animals feared. Snapping herself back to this unbelievable reality, she struggled harder, heart pumping, ears ringing. She had to get that necklace from Sinclair's pocket and disappear.

"Strike the colors," the captain ordered, all the wind his in proverbial sails gone.

"Sir?" Fergus asked, confused, and turned to see for himself.

The captain's intimidating posture slid away. This was one of defeat. "She's flying the black, and she's too fast to outrun. We're surrendering."

"But captain," Fergus protested. "Th'owners forbid such an act."

Another cannon boomed from the pirate ship, but this one crunched wood on impact.

"Would you prefer death to being discharged? Now do as you're told!"

Refusing to surrender to pirates was the equivalent of consenting to fight. Pirates chose nimble ships for their speed, and they carried many men and plenty of guns.

Merchant ships were the exact opposite—under-crewed, under-protected, and cumbersome to maneuver. Neither side wanted to fight. Pirates didn't want to take damage, and merchants didn't want to lose their trade goods. No one wanted a ship to repair either.

The smartest choice was to surrender, allow the pirates to take what they wanted and leave, but some weren't so amicable. The most ruthless would slaughter the crew for sport or spite. If Captain Sinclair's orders weren't followed quickly enough, the pirates just might make an example out of them.

Wild-eyed, Fergus rushed to lower the English flag. While the helmsman held the wheel steady with the wind, the rest of the crew joined the captain. Everyone huddled at the starboard side, watching their impending fate unfold.

Emily was helplessly forgotten at the mast.

The merchant crew numbered about a dozen and a half. As the pirate ship approached, their opponents lining the rail numbered over seventy, maybe eighty. Dirty, sweaty, leather-tanned faces snarled at them as the barque closed the distance.

Emily's heart pounded harder. Sweat beaded on her forehead and chest, and she fought her scratching binds like her life depended on it.

"Dear, god," Captain Sinclair whispered. "Lemoine's coming."

He and the crew scrambled away from the rail as grappling hooks soared through the sky, landing like a string of muffled gunshots. A charge was shouted, and dozens of pirates lowered gangplanks and crossed over. Some jumped on the rigging with cutlasses and pistols at the ready. The pirates swarmed the deck like locusts, encapsulating the merchant crew, ready to devour their prey.

Emily shivered, arms aching, wrists burning and bleeding, not wanting to believe any of this was real.

From the sea of filthy testosterone, a single pirate stepped forward and approached the merchant captain. He was dazzling and completely handsome. A friendly smile lit up his brown eyes, and sunlight glinted off a gold earring. A sexy, neatly trimmed beard gave him a ruggedness Emily hadn't seen outside of the movies. He stood a few inches taller than her five-foot-nine height, and while his hands were empty, a cutlass and pistol hung from a belt. This contrast to the rest of the crew led Emily to believe this man, wearing a dark cocked hat over wavy brown locks tied at the nape of his neck, was their captain. He oozed confidence, as if he owned all these men, and they'd run into the line of fire for him. Judging by their rough appearances, that was likely true.

Captain Donald Sinclair paled, and the pirate captain strutted over to him. The merchant captain displayed a gruesome personality on his sleeve. But the cheerfulness of the pirate captain made him more dangerous. He enjoyed stealing from others, inciting fear in their hearts, and terrifying their minds.

Emily had made too many mistakes in the man department. She would no longer be swayed by a pretty face. This one was a despicable thief and proud of it.

"Let me be first to thank you for surrendering, good sir. You have made the wise decision to save us bloodshed. I'm Captain Lemoine of the *Sea Lion*. While my crew searches your hold, I'll be the judge of your trial." His voice was smooth, charismatic, and lilted with a swoon-worthy French accent—a trifecta of danger.

The other crew members quickly relieved Sinclair of his goods, carrying the barrels from below deck across to the pirate ship. The quartermaster recorded the ill-gotten goods on paper.

"Trial?" the merchant captain repeated with raised brows. "I did nothing wrong. We surrendered. Take what you must and leave us in peace!"

Captain Lemoine shook his head with amusement. "That's not how this works." He signaled with a nod, and a handful of pirates captured Sinclair and dragged him toward Emily at the mast, but they paused and traded looks of confusion.

The brutish merchant captain stared Emily down with wild eyes. But he didn't apologize. She had nothing to say to him except, "Give me my necklace."

The anger returned to his features, and any sympathy Emily carried vanished.

"Captain?" one of Sinclair's captors prompted.

Pirate Captain Lemoine swaggered toward her and scratched as the scruff on his chin. Despite her much better judgment, Emily's heart sped up as he assessed her appearance, deep brown eyes raking her from head to toe and back. Heat sizzled—did he like what he saw? Because Captain Lemoine was very easy on the eyes, and if she had half of Angela's mind, she'd take him...

Captain Sinclair uttered a soft noise of terror, snapping her out of the ridiculous fantasy. The horrible brute was terrified of this handsome, charismatic pirate, so Emily's fear surged as Captain Lemoine reached her. Was he simply excited to decide on a new punishment for her?

"You, sailor, what have you done?" Captain Lemoine demanded with playful curiosity, while both merchant and pirate crews watched her.

But all Emily could see was Captain Lemoine. Up close, Emily guessed he was around forty years old and far too attractive for this vile life he lived. She glanced at Sinclair again for a reminder. Attractive or not, this pirate was not a knight in shining armor here to rescue her.

She had to stick to the plan—retrieve her necklace and find Angela. Then go home.

CAPTAIN ERIC LEMOINE NEEDED a win today. So far, things were looking better than average without any loss or damage to his ship. The crew secured their prize, and that meant he could keep his hide intact for one more account. Most of the time, Captain Lemoine dreaded the standard trial and torture of the rival captain, but not this time. Captain Donald Sinclair was a nasty fellow, and he deserved the darkest pain Lemoine could conjure from the bowels of the seas.

And he'd take pleasure in it.

But Captain Lemoine hadn't expected to interrupt a punishment in progress. The promise of disparaging Sinclair to his face lifted Lemoine's spirits beyond what he'd thought possible lately. He didn't need to don a facade at all for this. But when he'd laid eyes on the prisoner in question, Lemoine was taken aback. His focus shifted.

The prisoner's clothes looked proper, but there was something off about them. They were too clean. The materials were too new. The cut was custom-made. He appeared weaker than his counterparts, but yet well-nourished. And the prisoner's face was...stunning. There was a fire behind those smart eyes warring with terror. A spark of life unheard of among these seadogs. And mid-thirties in age, if he had to guess—not at all the usual range for sailors. This prisoner didn't seem to be a merchant sailor at all.

Lemoine didn't typically find himself fancying men, but there was something about this one that left him both puzzled and fascinated. He needed to know everything about him.

Scratching at his beard in amusement, Captain Lemoine repeated his demand, unsatisfied until it was answered, "Why are you tied to the mast?"

"The captain stole my necklace, but claimed I was the thief." The prisoner's voice was lighter than he'd expected, with almost a feminine lilt, and that excited Lemoine even more. This prisoner was certainly not like the others.

"Preposterous," the nasty fellow declared. "He's a stowaway and a thief!"

Ah, the heart of the accusation. One clearly punishable by whipping, but rather than dole out the earned punishment, Captain Lemoine's curiosity only grew. Instead of booking proper passage, this man stowed away, which could only lead Lemoine to believe this prisoner was on the run. He didn't want to be found. But why was a man running with a necklace, of all things?

"What does this necklace look like?" Captain Lemoine asked as a test of his powers of deduction. A liar wouldn't have specifics at the ready, and he hoped, for the prisoner's sake, the accusations were false. Not just because he wanted to slight the captain. Lemoine couldn't see himself harming this prisoner.

"It's amethyst on a copper chain, and it's still in his right pocket."

That was perfect. With a satisfactory grin, Captain Lemoine approached his rival and searched his pocket, revealing the gem matching the description.

"This the one?" Captain Lemoine asked, holding it for him to see.

"It is. Please give it back." His words were a gentle plea.

Captain Lemoine lifted up the symbol of innocence, and a noise of admiration followed. It wasn't for Lemoine's efforts to prove Sinclair's disturbing countenance. No, that was well known. The noise was for the appeared value of the gem. Likely stolen, and that was the reason the prisoner ran. Lemoine would free this prisoner, but he still wasn't satisfied.

Captain Lemoine tucked the necklace into his own breast pocket. Now the prisoner would not leave until Captain Lemoine was finished with him.

Chapter 5

Captain Lemoine was a pirate, so Emily shouldn't have been surprised by his actions. But since she'd asked nicely, she thought he'd be a decent person and hand it over. Instead, all the terror she might've entertained was smothered by fury. "That's mine! You can't take it," Emily shouted at his back.

Captain Lemoine turned and smiled. "You'll do well to thank me."

Emily flinched. "What? For what?"

Captain Lemoine gestured, and a pair of other men, not currently securing Captain Donald Sinclair, moved to the back of the mast and freed her. All the wind in her proverbial sails stalled out. At his shocking kindness, she was no longer irate, but she couldn't stomach gratitude. Emily rubbed her cracked and bleeding wrists.

Captain Lemoine closed the distance between them, and the scent of leather, salty sweat, and a splash of rum filled her nose. As she'd guessed, he stood a few inches taller than her, the perfect kissing height. "You're welcome," he said softly.

There was an intimacy in his tone, and Emily was speechless. She should've been afraid. She should've hated him. Logically, she should assault his person and forcibly take her necklace back, but she didn't. Emily stood inches from this man, his eyes memorizing every inch of her, while dozens of men watched. Captain Lemoine was no knight in shining armor, but he did save her.

Before Emily could ask for the necklace again, the captain casually gestured. This time, Captain Sinclair was tied to the mast, face outward, reminding Emily of this sexy man's incredible danger. With Captain's Lemoine's attention shifted, Emily melted into the remaining merchant crew, finding a small safety in Fergus's presence.

"What's going to happen?" she whispered.

Fergus bent down to her ear. "They're gunna give th'crew a chance tae make a case against th'captain, and if the pirate chooses, he'll kill him."

Emily was disgusted by the brute who intended to strip her half naked, whip her to within an inch of her life, and then...do whatever he wanted with a helpless woman. She couldn't watch, but she couldn't look away either. As much as she didn't condone this type of public display, she wanted to know what kind of person Captain Lemoine was. When he'd freed her, there was a spark between them. She was sure of it. But why did Captain Sinclair mumble his name in terror when the pirates approached?

Both crews formed a thick circle around the mast, but the pirates kept the merchant crew collected in a nervous group. Captain Lemoine paced and began his trial. "Merchant sailors! Has this man done you any wrongs?" The crew twitched and fidgeted, as if afraid of punishment for speaking out. Emily would've added her voice if her dilemma wasn't already known. "Has this captain been fair to you all? Rations plenty? Wages satisfactory?"

Fergus stepped forward. "When a storm hit, th'ship rocked tumultuously, an' I dropped a ration in th'mess, purely oan accident. But I ate it wi'out complaint. None was wasted at all. The captain declared me an inept, blundering fool, and I begged fur mercy under th'cat."

Fergus had implied he'd experienced the whip, but the irrational and excessive use of force still shocked her. The captain really was going to whip her just for possessing a necklace.

"Anyone else?" Captain Lemoine prompted.

Another man, more like a boy, stepped forward and cleared his throat. "Captain Sinclair docked my wages and removed my rations for two days, because I fell asleep on the night watch. I did mean to!"

"Fair enough," Captain Lemoine said as a means of accepting his testimony, not agreeing with the punishment given. "Any others? I want the full truth. And I promise no consequences shall befall any of you."

When the pirates swarmed over, cutlasses and pistols at the ready, she'd expected a bloodbath, not a fair trial. Emily was baffled at the kindness shown to the merchant crew.

"Aye, sir," a deeper voice came from the crowd, and a hefty man stepped forward. "I was repairing a hole in the hull, but the hammer smarted my thumb, and I shouted, disturbing the captain's rest. He took a cane to the back of my head." The crewman swiped the wound, and brown matted blood crusted on his fingers, proving his tale, and showing it happened very recently.

"I never...!" Captain Sinclair shouted.

At the cowardly protest, Captain Lemoine gripped the pistol from his waist belt and fired a single shot into Sinclair's gut. The brute moaned in agony.

Emily startled at the noise and covered her open mouth with her hand, but the crew around her remained calm, even Fergus. Captain Lemoine just...he just...shot the man, and no one seemed to care. That shot wouldn't kill Sinclair for a while. It wasn't meant to be a quick execution.

Captain Lemoine tucked his expended weapon back in his belt where he stored it. "Gentlemen, an easy choice awaits you. Stay here and secure your fate with this wicked captain, or join us aboard the *Sea Lion*." The captain made eye contact with each man as if everyone's decision was important, but when it was Emily's turn, he lingered. Her heart leaped into her throat.

His voice carried. "If you want nothing to do with our crew, we will happily deposit you in Nassau to find your own way home."

The merchant crew mumbled among themselves. Fergus stayed silent, as did Emily.

"But, if you choose to sign the articles of agreement, you'll find yourself bestowed with more riches than any merchant crewman could dream of. We may have declared war against the world, but on our ship, all men are equals. One vote each, no matter his station. What say you?"

The merchant crew huddled together as if making the choice as one. They quietly argued, debating both sides. Some readily wanted to join the crew, while others wanted to go home. Fergus still remained silent.

Emily would not stay and die like the animal shot and tied to the mast. She had a necklace to retrieve, a friend to find, and a festival to get back to. That meant she had to follow Captain Lemoine, but men didn't treat women kindly aboard ships. And every passing minute had her worrying more for Angela. So Emily had to assert herself as one of them.

Emily broke from the murmurs of the merchant group and approached Lemoine, head held high, but her heart pounded in her chest the closer she got. The last person who argued with this handsome man received a fatal wound in the gut. "I'm Porter. Emile Porter, and I choose to accept your gracious offer to board the *Sea Lion*. But my companion, Angela, is missing. Can I search for her before we leave?"

Captain Lemoine smiled and scratched at his beard again. Emily wanted to run her fingers through it. Catching herself staring at his hands, she focused on his dark eyes. That wasn't much better. "Price?"

Emily was lost. She thought the offer was free, and the only thing of value she had, he'd already stolen. "Pardon?"

"Sir?" A man approached with a clipboard. The quartermaster. He wore his hair in a long braid down his back, and his clothing was almost as fancy as the captain's—a long dark coat with gold buttons over his breeches and tunic.

"Has anyone found a woman below deck?"

Price scowled. "I would've heard of it." He had a charming British accent, but his clear distaste for women turned her off, even though she expected such a response.

"Angela isn't here? You're certain?"

Price swung his eyes to her. "We would never leave behind a prize such as that."

No kidding. Emily nodded, accepting his answer, and Captain Lemoine gestured for her to cross a gangplank to his ship. "Wise choice, sailor."

Emily approached the plank, not realizing until this moment she was slightly afraid of heights. Hugging a crow's nest with the safety of modern equipment was different to traipsing on a rocking, unsecured slab of wood between two moving ships over two dozen feet in the air.

If she fell, she could swim, but that wouldn't do her much good if the hulls crushed her.

Emily shivered and held out her arms for balance as she crossed the unstable plank. After her feet landed on pirate territory, Emily exhaled in relief. Fergus hopped down behind her. Then more continued until all the dozen or so men climbed over. Pirates returned, filling the deck and beginning the slow process of setting sail once again.

"Will ye be signing?" Fergus asked in private.

Emily wasn't remotely attracted to the lanky younger man, but she could listen to him speak forever. "I'm going to do whatever it takes to get my necklace back."

"It's that important tae ye?"

"It's all I know." Emily didn't realize how much she appreciated the mundane of home until now.

A handful of remaining pirates carried barrels on their shoulders and settled them around Captain Donald Sinclair. Cries of mercy floated over from the merchant ship.

"Are they doing what I think they're doing?" Emily asked her new friend, nerves spearing through her. She'd trusted Quartermaster Price when he said Angela wasn't there. But there's a finality in what was happening. No more chances to be sure. But if she and Angela put on the necklaces together, and Angela wasn't here, where did her best friend go?

"Appears tae be so. Canny say I'll miss it."

One final barrel was unsealed and spilled in a long trail around the deck.

Captain Lemoine returned to his ship and shouted gleefully, "Weigh anchor, and we'll continue the account as planned."

While the crew set to work, knowing what to do, the man with the barrel tossed the empty away and lit the black path of gunpowder. The grappling hooks were cut free, and the ship drifted with the tug of the wind.

Captain Donald Sinclair's cries for mercy were carried away by the breeze. After a short distance, flames hungry for the gunpowder engulfed the deck. A thunderous explosion sent debris and splinters of wood soaring through the clear sky. Emily ducked below the bulwark, eyes wide, and checked the other men for their reactions. No one cared.

Except Captain Lemoine watched with his hands clasped behind his back, grinning.

The brutish captain went down with the two halves of his ship.

6

Chapter 6

IN THE MESS BELOW deck, candlelight flickered on long tables while high-spirited men told tall tales. Their peals of laughter and sloshing drinks lifted Emily's lips. She and the merchant crew were perched at the end of a table, a place for guests, while the pirate crew spread out. The atmosphere reminded her of a dingy neighborhood bar filled with old friends, but in desperate need of ventilation.

Surprisingly, the pirates were hospitable, offering biscuit and drinks. But this...This required a strong stomach and weak tongue to swallow without gagging. The smell alone was enough to make her want to dive into the ocean and hope for the best. She would've felt slighted, but everyone ate and drank alike. The captain had been truthful, thus far.

Her thoughts drifted back to the brutish captain, whose end was violent and abrupt. Angela had accompanied her on the replica ship, but her date was supposed to be Tyler. Skipping the part where her ex-boyfriend wouldn't buy or wear a necklace, Emily mused if Tyler had been on that ship with her, he'd have wet his pants facing Sinclair.

Like Captain Lemoine, Tyler was a smooth-talker, but unlike the captain, Tyler was all talk, a chicken under those pretty feathers. Picturing it literally, Emily chuckled. Now she wished he had joined her, if only so she could give him an ultimatum—return all her money and apologize until she was satisfied, or stay here forever.

"What could possibly amuse ye at a time like this?" Fergus whispered. He hadn't been amused by the camaraderie down here. If he hadn't told his tale of being whipped, Emily would've believed Fergus preferred to stay with the merchant ship.

"Personal thoughts, that's all."

Fergus swallowed a draft from his cup while staring at her in thought. Emily shifted uncomfortably in her seat, wishing he'd look anywhere else. So far, no one questioned her being Emile, and she couldn't afford suspicion.

"How did a merchant sailor come tae possess a necklace o' such rare beauty?"

Emily blinked. She hadn't expected to explain herself, so she concocted a memorable fib. "My sister gifted it to me, so I could sustain myself once I reached the mainland. I couldn't find a buyer willing to offer a fair price, and I wasn't going to cut it into pieces. So I hid aboard the merchant ship for a trip to Florida."

Fergus smiled. "Ye did stowaway."

Heat crept up her cheeks once again. "Were you really going to cut off my jerkin?"

Fergus bit off a crunchy piece of biscuit and spoke with his mouth full. "Nae one deliberately defies the captain. But I've bin sailing th'seas aboard a merchant ship since I was but a wee lad, so I can assure ye, whatever these scoundrels would dae is much worse than Captain Sinclair."

Emily had observed just the opposite—fairness and a chance to defend oneself. "If that's the case, then why had

Captain Lemoine treated your crew so well? Why didn't he just kill us all after taking what he wanted?"

Fergus's lips thinned, and Emily had no idea why she was defending them—the pirate captain shot the merchant captain for no reason and taken her necklace. She chewed her hard biscuit, avoiding Fergus's judgmental gaze.

A loud banging at the head of the table, like a sword's hilt against the hardwood, silenced the room. Captain Lemoine addressed all hands. "To our new friends, welcome aboard." He lifted a cup and drank to his short toast, and the pirate crew followed suit with cheery hollers.

Listening to his lilting French accent, Emily bit back a smile. There was something about him. Every time Captain Lemoine spoke, he commanded the room, and no one else existed but him.

When the crew settled, Captain Lemoine continued his grand speech. "We have been accused of being dirty thieves, but the hypocrisy is right in front of you. The Crown itself takes and takes and gives nothing in return. Merchant ship captains treat you no better than slaves in their hold—shorting wages, withholding rations, the constant threat of the cat."

Murmurs of agreement came from the merchant sailors, and Emily was enthralled with his defense of being a thief. Tyler denied what he'd done and played stupid. Captain Lemoine was admitting it and explaining his actions. She might not approve of what he'd done, but she could respect his stance.

"But as you sit before me, you're free from those chains. Now I offer you something more. Aboard the *Sea Lion*, all men have an equal vote and a fair share in rations and prizes. Tired of being hungry? Tired of being broke? The right prize can award more dollars than a year's salary!"

The men murmured again, dazzled by the promises of riches. Emily wasn't on board. What good was living a life of luxury when all you did was take someone else's? There was no honor in that. And since it involved taking other ships by force and risking one's life, Emily was definitely not interested. And on top of that, injuries and deaths were so common, Captain Lemoine thanked the merchant crew for sparing the pirates that usual fate. There was her final 'no thanks'.

"You'd be foolish to turn your back on this opportunity. With that in mind, you can decide on your future right now. Remain merchant sailors, where your careers shall be tarnished when word returns of your surrender to pirates. You'll be begging for a new assignment, and if you find one, suffer with pitiful wages." The captain paused for effect and the pirates jeered and pounded their cups on the tables.

The captain flashed his radiant smile, and his gaze lingered on Emily. Was he trying to tell her which option he wanted her to choose? Her heart skipped a beat at the decision she'd already made.

His gaze moved away. "Or sign the accords and be rich and free, because aboard the *Sea Lion*, we are all free men!"

The pirates cried out in celebration, rattling their cups, and drumming palms on the tables like a marching band. Their excitement was contagious. Emily smiled.

"Ye no' seriously considering this hogwash?" Fergus asked. The scowl on his face made it clear the captain hadn't won him over.

"It's pretty convincing to me."

Fergus scoffed. "How could ye? Look at them—a pack o' animals—brutes, thieves, murderers, enemies tae th'Crown. Ye want th'threat o' a noose over yer head every day? Th'worry about th'next sails ye see being th'Royal Navy's? Th'fear yer next battle ends in miserable bloodshed and prolonged agony o' mortal wounds? I'm staying oan th'good side o' the law, an' I advise ye tae refuse."

His arguments didn't make sense to her. "As a merchant sailor in pirate-infested waters, aren't you exposed to all those same concerns, except for the noose?"

Fergus studied his cup. "Ma conscious is clear."

Unsatisfied with his answer, Emily pressed, "You'd rather endure abuse and starvation from a merchant captain than live the freedoms of a pirate?" Captain Lemoine explained they weren't simply thieves. They were taking back what the Crown had taken from them. And that Emily could understand—as she gazed longingly at the captain and wondered which pocket her necklace rested in. The pirates took what they needed and freed men from worse situations. They didn't want to hurt anyone. They weren't the monsters depicted in the books. They were angry men without hope.

Of course she had to sign. She'd do whatever it took to get that necklace back. Besides, if she chose to disembark at Nassau, what kind of life could she make for herself? As a retail worker used to electronic inventory systems and monitoring the self-checkouts, she had no relevant job skills here. She had friends and family to return to, and an ex-boyfriend to hound for her money back. The only way back to her life was to join these pirates.

Fergus didn't answer her question before a rhythmic pounding on the long table reached an excited commotion, drowning out all other sounds. Captain Lemoine beamed from the support and gestured at a small table with a parchment, quill, and inkwell lit with candles. The quartermaster stood next to him, holding a clipboard.

The pirate crew stood with ceremony and lined up against the wall. The defeated crew was urged to sign with continued vocalizations in support.

The merchant crew stood one by one and in pairs, and lined up at the table.

Emily joined them, hanging at the back of the line, wanting to watch the others first. With each signature, the captain smiled, patted the recruit on the back, and said something to him, inaudible over the cheers. The line progressed smoothly until Fergus, who was ahead of her. Rather than take up the quill, he approached the captain and said, "I mean nae insult, but I canny, in good conscience, sign. I'll disembark safely at Nassau, as promised."

The quartermaster made notes on his paperwork, unflinching at the refusal. But Emily focused on the captain as firelight danced across his strong features. He showed no signs of insult. He didn't try to sway him further. The captain respected Fergus's decision.

"As you wish," the captain replied.

Emily pressed a finger to her lips to stifle a chuckle at the captain's use of Westley's declaration of love for his dearest Buttercup.

Captain Lemoine turned his attention to her and raised a brow, but he wasn't upset with her. He was curious. "Is something the matter, Porter?"

There was so much the matter, Emily didn't know where to begin.

Chapter 7

THE ENTIRE COMPANY OF pirates stared at Emily, but the only one whose scrutinizing gaze sent waves of nerves through her stomach was Captain Lemoine himself. Or maybe the biscuit didn't agree with her. Could be that, too.

"No. Nothing's the matter at all. Please continue." Emily said, face burning hot. Sweat trickled down her back.

The captain returned to Fergus and said, "Your needs shall be met until port, and until then, no harm to your person shall transpire."

With a quiet audience, her friend nodded and stepped aside, satisfied with the promises. Two more men declined to sign, and Emily stepped up to the table next to the captain, staring her down. Her heart thundered in her chest, and blood wooshed in her ears. He stared back, but there was a softness in his eyes—not the hard angles of a dominant male asserting his position. This was a man silently pleading with her to sign.

Had he figured out she was a woman?

The pirates remained quiet while Emily made her choice. She bent over the parchment and the cursive handwriting flickering by candlelight was beautiful. Had the captain penned this himself? A real life article of agreement, the pirate code, right in front of her. This belonged in a museum. She was afraid of touching it and having the delicate paper crumble—but it was new, not an antique.

If she signed, would her name appear in history?

Emily blinked. Everyone was watching. She couldn't take the time for an existential crisis. Down to business.

The first articles were expected—*equal vote in all affairs, and a fair turn in all prizes. No gambling or theft amongst the crew. Extinguish lights and drinking at night. And pistols and cutlasses in working and ready order at all times.* Surprisingly civil.

After that, Emily grew concerned. *No one breaks up the account until each man has earned 1,000.* Her face pinched in confusion. A thousand days of service? A thousand dollars? Emily wasn't familiar with their standards, but she had no intention of sticking around that long. She wanted complete clarification before signing a contract—she'd learned the hard way to protect herself—but she didn't think the captain would like her questioning. And Emily couldn't draw attention to herself more than necessary.

A quarrel on the ship is settled on shore by sword or pistol. Emily made a note to avoid all confrontation.

Refraining from battle is punished by death. So if the captain chose battle, she could die, and if she chose not to partake, she'd be killed. That was...not fair. How much worse could this get?

"Something the matter?" Captain Lemoine asked.

Emily straightened, quill in her hand. "I'm just reading it first. The handwriting is beautiful."

The captain grinned, sending her heart fluttering. "How are you not familiar with the articles? Everyone at sea knows them."

"I'm new," Emily said, and bent back down. Faster. She needed to go faster. She skimmed ahead and immediately regretted it. Emily re-read the passage, disbelieving her own eyes. *No fornication or women on board, and any caught are to suffer death.*

She'd known women weren't treated well, but *death?* This was an oppressive world, far removed from what she was familiar with. No amount of reading passages in books, translated and pieced together over centuries, could prepare someone to experience it. And even though her country had many social issues, she was thankful something this brutal wasn't one of them.

If Emily didn't sign, she'd be removed from the ship at Nassau, leaving her with a very narrow window to coax her necklace back. Otherwise, she'd remain trapped here forever. She truly had no choice. She just had to not get caught. Surely the captain didn't already know her secret and was allowing her to sign her own death sentence, right?

Emily peeked up at the captain.

A bell chimed above deck, and Emily whipped her head around in alarm. Another ship? Another battle? Good thing she hadn't signed yet. She silently searched the captain's reaction, hoping for reassurance.

He tilted his head at her quizzically.

"Seven bells. You know your places," a man said.

Emily turned. Several men quietly left the mess, disappointment on their faces. That man must've been the boatswain, in charge of the hull, rigging, cables, and deck crew. A few of the shift-change men mumbled about Karl interrupting their fun. And still, these witnesses waited for her. Emily swallowed a thick lump in her throat.

IN ALL HIS YEARS freeing sailors from their wretched fates, Captain Eric Lemoine had never once encountered a man so unsure of this decision. So unfamiliar with the rules before him.

Who was Emile Porter?

Why did the shift change bells alarm him so? Why did he still hesitate to sign? Either he went with the rest of the crew who refused, or he joined us. The choice wasn't *that* difficult.

Emile bent down toward the parchment again, and a different possibility struck him. Could this man not read? Pity filled him at once. Captain Lemoine had been raised in privilege with the best education available, but he'd chosen this life.

It wasn't forced upon him.

And he, along with the original crew he'd rounded up, drafted these articles together. And yes, he'd written this—and re-written it with each new crew turnover.

"Shall I read it to you?" Captain Lemoine asked quietly.

Emile straightened, red burning on his smooth cheeks. The man was a master at shaving so close to the skin. His bright blond hair wouldn't have been enough to disguise it. No, this unusual and perplexing man was a master with a blade. Someone not to trifle with; someone Lemoine wanted close.

Captain Lemoine cared not what lied beneath Emile's breeches and tunic. He cared what lied inside that fascinating mind, and that desire led him to Emile's lips. Captain Lemoine wanted to kiss him.

Emile's gaze lingered on his lips as well, but then they tracked low and remained for long enough to tell Lemoine what he wanted to know. The captain's interest was reciprocated.

"See something you like?" he asked quietly.

Emile flustered, tipping his face away, bitting his lips. And that amusing blush returned to his cheeks. Emile wiped his palms on his breeches and smiled. His teeth were beautifully white and perfectly straight. He came from money too. "I was just thinking, but I'm ready now."

With a trembling hand, Emile lifted the quill and dipped it in the inkwell. He moved very slowly over to the parchment, and a drop of ink landed spilled.

"Oh, shit." Emile swiped at the stain, but it was going anywhere.

Captain Lemoine hid his amusement. This man had never used a quill before. How strange!

Finally, the signature scratched onto the parchment. Emile straightened, set down the quill, and squared his shoulders, lips pressed thin and cheeks burning bright.

He was staying.

The captain beamed and clapped the man on the back. "Congratulations, Emile. Nothing to fear, no? If you need any assistance in understanding the contract you signed, please do ask. My door is always open." The captain let that statement hang for a beat.

Emile blinked silently, as if not understanding.

Captain Lemoine needed to be more straightforward with this one. He leaned in close enough to feel his body heat, and the scent of this man puzzled him further. What sailor smelled like...flowers? "Welcome aboard, Emile Porter. You made the right choice."

Emile smiled, capturing the captain's full attention as he addressed the whole room, "Rum all around. Allow us to celebrate the new arrivals properly!"

A violin played an upbeat tune, and the men cheered and danced. A handful rushed to the cask and pried it open, and many swarmed it, scooping out the sloshing rum. Emile stayed behind. Captain Lemoine was thrilled for a chance to talk in private.

The quartermaster, always so serious, crossed the room and said in confidence, "Eric, we don't have enough rum for a full round."

The man needed to lighten up. For someone who knew the ins and outs of the ship and its finances, one would expect he could assuredly enjoy himself from time to time. The situation on the ship wasn't *that* dire. "How can you say we don't have enough? We raided a merchant ship, Price! What was the take?"

"Slops for half the men. Twenty barrels of sugar...."

"Sugar has considerable value."

Price wasn't convinced. "When sold at port, I agree, but we're far from port now." The man flipped pages and referenced his paperwork. "And we gained enough leather Monmouth caps for the whole crew."

That sounded like the entirety of the list, and that was terrible news. Lemoine grimly looked at his elated crew. "No more rum?"

"It pains me to say, but no. The sooner we make port, the sooner we can replenish our stores and our pockets. You have to keep them together until then."

No easy feat. "Can you dilute the remaining supply?"

"Do you think you can fool these men? Be careful, Eric." Price shook his head and retreated from the celebration.

Suddenly, Lemoine was no longer in the mood to celebrate.

Emile approached, and Lemoine could sense the man everywhere he stood. His presence alone pulled him from the melancholy problem before him.

"May I have a word with you, sir, privately?" Emile asked.

Captain Lemoine smiled. He needed a pleasant distraction, and he could think of none better. He hooked his arm behind the handsome man and walked him toward the deck. "Tonight is your night."

EMILY WAS KEENLY AWARE of the captain's presence at her side, the feel of his arm behind her. She was worried he'd accidentally touch something that gave her away. But she didn't want distance between them.

They climbed the ladder to the main deck, and Emily gasped at the clear sky, spinning in place with her head tilted back. She'd never seen an unimpeded view of the stars, free from untold numbers of satellites, rocket debris, and airplanes. With a smile on her face, she rushed to the rail and leaned over. Moonlight glinted and shimmered off the gently lapping ocean waters. And the quiet. She'd never experienced a relaxing peace like this. Nature just as nature intended.

The world seemed endless from here, blackness in every direction. No cruise liners, no speedboats, no flashing lights from lighthouses. It was more beautiful than she'd ever imagined.

"It's as if you've never seen the sky before," the captain mused.

Emily spun at his words. The captain was leaning against the rail, intently watching her.

"This is beautiful," she said without thinking.

"It is, isn't it?" The captain straightened and strolled toward her. "When the crew enjoys their drink, I step out here. I prefer the fresh air over the pungent lower deck."

Emily laughed. "Pungent is accurate."

The captain smiled, intense gaze assessing her. Emily covered her arms over her chest, pretending to be chilled. She definitely wasn't.

"An extra pair of eyes watching the horizon doesn't hurt. Not all ships move with light shining through their portholes." He leaned in close, and for a flash, Emily worried he was going to confront her over her grave mistake—signing as a woman. He said, "Don't tell the others, but I know the crow's nest sometimes dozes off."

Emily relaxed and joked, "Since you have a healthy-sized crew, I'm guessing you don't kill them as a punishment for it." She covered her mouth with her hand. That was distasteful and rude. But she was curious about the truth of her assumption.

Captain Lemoine tapped his nose with a spark in his eye. He seemed like a decent guy, but then why shoot another captain and burn him alive before blowing his ship to smithereens?

Needing an explanation, she asked, "Why did you do it?"

The captain folded his arms across his chest, smile fading away. "To what do you refer?"

Emily rubbed the gentle night breeze from her arms. This time, the chill reached her skin. "Captain Sinclair was immobilized on a ship doomed to be destroyed. Why did you bother to shoot him first? Doesn't it seem...I don't know...barbaric?"

Captain Lemoine squinted at her. "I understand the concern you carry for your captain. Being free can be hard to adjust to. What do you do now? Where do you go? How will you sustain yourself?"

"It's not that."

"But you signed, so you have no worries about any of that. On my crew, you'll be taken care of. The code we agreed to is binding for all and strictly enforced."

Emily dropped her eyes. She figured as much.

"That was supposed to bring consolation, but I sense it hasn't." Captain Lemoine touched her shoulder, exploring the handiwork of her jerkin. Her stomach tightened with unease. "Your clothing is familiar, but the fabrics and stitches are not. In all my years exploring this vast globe, your speech patterns are completely unrecognizable. I found you on a merchant ship, yet you behave like you've never seen the ocean. Your smooth skin tells me you're a master of the blade, but your nervousness tonight makes no sense. Please tell me, satisfy this deep yearning to understand, where are you from, Emile Porter?"

Emily backed toward the rail. He was too close, his suspicions too high. She couldn't fail already, so she spun his questions back at him while offering a taste of satisfaction. "Sinclair wasn't my captain, but you figured that much. Now, Captain Lemoine, satisfy my deep yearning to understand." She playfully used his words against him. "Your crew steals from honest merchants, destroying the livelihood of the sailors. As judge, jury, and executioner, you have no qualms about killing people. That tells me the stories of pirates are true." The captain closed the distance again, slowly, like a stalker in the night. He didn't like what she was saying. "But you freed the crews from tyrannical captains. And you offer them safe passage or a chance to join as equals with no questions asked. That altruism...that generous regard for others doesn't fit the profile. I cannot make sense of you."

The captain smiled under the moonlight and leaned in close. "If that was your attempt to quell my curiosity, you failed."

Emily had to be more blunt. "If I don't fit in here, then teach me, starting with explaining why you shot the captain, so I understand exactly what I signed up for."

Captain Lemoine scratched at his beard. Emily wanted to run her fingers through the short scruff, but she would never risk it. Not even if the captain had a good explanation for such a monstrous, tasteless, unnecessary act. "Trust is a valuable commodity aboard this ship."

Emily had already given her trust to the wrong people. Every little girl trusted her father to be loving, and always there. He had been the first to break it. She'd tried again as an adult, capable of choosing who she wanted to trust, and

Tyler was a bust too. They appeared decent people on the outside.

Regardless of his benevolent intentions, how could she trust someone who proudly proclaimed to be a murderer and a thief?

Angry men wearing frowns and shouting incoherently spilled onto the deck, interrupting their conversation. As if she'd been discovered, Emily stepped away, trembling like a leaf in the breeze, but the mob closed in around them both.

8

Chapter 8

WITHIN MOMENTS OF THE captain telling her he'd take care of her, Emily and Captain Lemoine were surrounded. Shouts demanded answers that Emily believed wouldn't be appeased with simple words of encouragement. Emily also didn't believe the captain would protect her, because she was just another one of the crew. Seeing a narrow opportunity, she sidled closer to the captain, anyway. If any of these angry pirates caused a shoving match, Emily planned to be close enough to dig in the captain's pockets without him realizing.

It was a terrible plan, but the only one she had.

"Captain," a filthy man said with a scowl. "Price says no more rum. Can I wager why he cut us off after *you* told the whole crew to indulge?"

"Simply my mistake," the captain placed a fist over his heart in solidarity. "I believed the stores to be in fine order, but Price's documents show otherwise."

Unsatisfied, he leaned closer. "According to the articles, we can vote on a retrenchment."

"You are within your rights to do so, but the outcome doesn't change the quantity left. You can drink it all down tonight and hope we don't suffer a thirst, or you can ration it out until we reach port."

The pirate thought on it for a beat. Others around murmured their opinions. "How long until we restock? Are we talking weeks or months?"

Wait, months? Emily needed enough time for her escape, but to be stuck here with these unstable cretins for months was...terrifying.

"Worry not. We must unload the sugar in Nassau to make room in the hold, and our guests who chose not to sign shall disembark. Soon we shall make landfall."

The explanation sounded reasonable to Emily, but she was curious what they needed room for.

"It's just like you to make promises, but failure after failure is all we see," the pirate continued, and others nodded and mumbled in agreement.

"I understand your disappointment—all of you." The captain turned, addressing glaring pairs of eyes. "But this afternoon's prize was unscheduled and came at no cost but time. I want to celebrate our unexpected good fortune, but the situation at hand requires patience."

"Patience!" another man hollered. "We don't want none of your patience. We want drinks!"

Emily made a mental note to never anger a half-drunk crowd.

"I bet the captain's keeping it all to himself!" another voice shouted. "Supposed to be equals, yet look at his clothes, and look at ours. He's got a cabin. We sleep in hammocks, shoulder to shoulder. He gets two shares of the prize, while we get one. What's fair about that?"

Emily understood higher pay for higher skilled positions with more responsibility, and it wasn't like the captain and his officers received a hundred shares over the workers.

With their pay, they could spend on their choice of clothing, but she had nothing to defend the cabin. With the whole ship ganging up on him, a thread of pity wove through her. Despite not knowing the man and having witnessed him shooting a man for suffering's sake, she believed his words were sincere. Emily didn't want to see the captain harmed, but what could she do against all of them?

A hand gripped Emily's arm and tugged. She allowed herself to be pulled from the mob and was surprised to see Fergus. "What are you doing?" she asked sharply, having lost her chance to frisk the captain.

"Getting ye out o' there. An angry crew ainlie leads tae one thing."

Emily stared, assuming he was going to finish. She prompted him, "Well, what? What is it?"

Fergus cocked his head as if puzzled why she wouldn't know and said, "Mutiny. An' if they succeed, th'captain's previous orders be nullified."

"Meaning, your safe passage is at stake?"

Fergus nodded. "An' ma two friends, who also declined th'crew's offer."

Emily couldn't afford to lose the captain. From what she'd heard, they could simply tip him overboard. It was an extreme solution, but Emily didn't know these people, and the captain seemed nervous and unsuccessful in placating the mob. She needed something, anything, that would calm them down. The crew suspected the captain had a spare barrel for his private use. Could Price be wrong about his count? It was the only idea she had, and she needed muscles to help. Fergus wouldn't be her first choice for the job, but she'd take what she could get. "Fergus, you need the captain to stay in charge for a little while longer, just as I do. Come help me before we're too late."

Emily headed down the ladder below deck.

Fergus followed curiously. "Wi' what?"

Emily remembered schematics of ships in her research. The hold was always below deck, and this ship wasn't that big. Inside, she found all the barrels taken from the merchant captain, as well as the pirates' meager stores.

"Find some liquor, any liquor. There's got to be a discrepancy here."

"An' if we're caught?"

"Act crazy, and I'll tell them I followed you for your safety." Emily systematically opened barrels and checked their contents.

Fergus folded his arms across his narrow chest. "Ye want me tae cover for ye? Ye know how this looks? Stealing from pirates is the worst offense. It was in the articles ye signed."

"The more you balk instead of help, the longer this takes."

Fergus sighed and opened barrels. Emily moved from one to the next. After clearing most of the hold, Emily found one barrel that might work. She leaned down for a quick whiff, and her eyes watered—not from the strength, but from the stink. This was the stuff.

She shouted louder than she'd planned, "I found one!"

Emily replaced the lid carefully, and Fergus fished his way over. She assessed her friend's strength. "Can you carry it?"

Fergus frowned. "Why? Canny ye?"

Uh, no. She couldn't. Emily stared, pleading with her friend.

Fergus scrutinized her appearance again, and Emily wished he wouldn't be suspicious. "Then why are ye insulting ma person?" he asked playfully and picked it up with ease. "Of course I can."

On their way back up to the main deck, Emily kept watch for Price, but the lower decks were vacant. Emily urged Fergus to hurry. "You first. You're carrying the precious cargo." Emily climbed up behind him, and Fergus set the barrel down on the main deck. The pirates shouted among themselves, as if the crew had split their loyalty. She wasn't too late.

Fergus backed away. Clearly, he didn't want credit for helping the crew.

"Hey! Anyone want a drink?" Emily shouted and slapped her hand on the wooden lid for their attention.

All the men ignored her, unable to hear over their own noise. Frustrated, Emily waved her arms like a cheerleader and shouted again. Still nothing. Emily marched up to the first pirate and pulled on his arm. "I have liquor over there!" She pointed and quickly, more heads turned.

The bickering quieted down, and with last glares and pats on the back, the men surrounded the barrel, many with empty cups still in their hands. They lifted the barrel and carried it down to the mess, song returning to their lips and cheerfulness returning to their countenances.

Fergus followed them with a last glance over his shoulder at her. He wasn't grateful, but he wasn't angry. There was a sadness on his features. Why on earth would he be sad his protection was no longer threatened?

The captain waited until they were alone. This time, his playfulness was gone. His features were darkened by the shadows cast by the moon. "Where did you find that rum?"

Emily shivered at the menace in his tone.

CAPTAIN ERIC LEMOINE HAD been as careful as possible with the crew lately. He knew the prizes hadn't been satisfactory, and the last one was pure happenstance. If they'd taken damage, he feared he wouldn't be captain at all right now. He never thought he'd want to thank old Captain Sinclair for his cowardice.

The rum situation was, as they'd said, more akin to a straw that broke a camel's back. But Emile Porter blew that straw away before the irreparable damage had been done. The question was, how? Emile already filled Lemoine's thoughts with the unanswered puzzle, and now Emile went and did this. But the man didn't carry confidence in his decision as he should have. It was reckless and impulsive.

Emile Porter was afraid.

"The hold," he said softly.

Lemoine dragged a hand down his face. "Quartermaster Price is going to have your head."

Emile gasped and covered his mouth with his hand. He truly knew nothing of our seafaring ways. Captain Lemoine bit back a chuckle at the perceived literal sense of his statement. Because of Emile's imbecilic decision, Lemoine lived another day, and that gratitude needed to be expressed. A simple 'thank you' would do nothing to prevent the due punishment. Considering Quartermaster Price was as rigid as a charred rabbit over a spit, that was no easy feat at all. Lemoine said gently, "But you saved mine."

"You're not mad?" Emile asked.

Lemoine tilted his head at her. "Do I appear unhinged? I thought my arguments were plain. And now I'm reminded of your strangeness. Can you offer me one answer?"

Emile's breath caught. "Sure."

Captain Lemoine grinned hungrily, as if a treasure of his own, dangling beyond reach, at last had been offered. He closed the distance between them until the man stood within inches of his chest. Lemoine wanted to reach out and capture the man's smooth jaw between his hands, and he wanted to taste the curve of Emile's upper lip. Which truthfully surprised him, but when Lemoine wanted something, he didn't abstain...

...except the articles forbade such actions.

"Where are you from, Emile?" he asked in almost a whisper. He thought it was a simple question, one easily answered, and one that would satisfy a miniscule piece of the puzzle.

Emile hesitated. "I'm not from around here."

Captain Lemoine tried to hide his disappointment. A captain and his crew needed trust to operate smoothly and safely. But having his newest recruit choose a lie by omission was more than just a chink in the chain. It stung. And that reminded him of the problem Emile had caused. "Indeed. Well, Porter, despite your benevolent efforts, I find myself in an unsatisfactory situation."

"What do you mean?"

Lemoine crossed his arms over his chest, the desire to retaliate for the personal slight taking over. "You subverted my authority in front of the crew."

Emile stepped back, and as the words sank into that pretty blond head of his, he frowned. His words came out unsure at first, then grew with assertiveness. "I...I did what I had to. I heard the crew was going to mutiny. Without me, you'd have no authority left to defend."

Lemoine admitted to himself he had a point. But Emile's actions left him with different problems. And yet the puzzle remained. "All actions have consequences."

Emile's boldness washed away, and the fear returned. He rubbed his arms as if chilled. "Am I going to be punished?"

"The crew, no doubt, shall delight in telling the story, and the quartermaster shall catch wind of it. He alone decides the punishments as set forth in the articles, but Price is not well liked by the crew. He's a decent man, it's simply the requirements of the job. I may be able to negotiate a mercy."

"I don't know how to thank you enough."

"Don't thank me yet."

"I'm sorry for what happened. I didn't know." Emile swiped his forehead.

"I believe you," Captain Lemoine said. "I wish I knew how it was possible."

Emile's drawn face shifted away. He gazed at the sea once again, lost in thought. Lemoine didn't guarantee a stay of punishment, because he couldn't. But the perplexing man only tried to help. To ease the burden of waiting for news, Captain Lemoine could offer him a small peace. "If the time comes, I owe you a personal favor."

Captain Lemoine hoped that wasn't another mistake. He turned and headed for his cabin across the deck before another word was spoken. Convincing the quartermaster of anything was a difficult task.

Chapter 9

IN THE SMALL MORNING hours, Emily opened her eyes. Despite all the worries on her mind, the soft movement of the ship and its rhythmic clicks and groans had lulled her to sleep. Overhead, thick wood beams ran from port to starboard. She was on the gun deck, in a sea of canvas hammocks swaying as one. She rubbed the sleep from her eyes. Her wild adventure had not been a hallucination.

Which was both exciting and incredibly terrifying.

Emily had wanted to cash in on the favor immediately, but the captain had marched away and disappeared behind a door before she could ask. He had a lot on his mind, and she didn't blame him. Emily had read the articles clearly before signing, but she didn't know what Price would charge her with.

Marooning was a death sentence—being left on an uninhabited island to die of thirst. That was three days of torture with an end in sight. She couldn't risk getting the cat. The whip alone was horrific but survivable. She was more afraid of being stripped half naked, of being exposed to several dozen men starved for something that wasn't food. That was a torture with no end.

While the pirates snored soundly, now was her best chance of escaping. Placing her feet on the deck, Emily carefully slipped out of the moving bed and tip-toed down the narrow space. She found a quick path across the gun deck and moved swiftly. Climbing the ladder to the main deck, she craned her neck, seeking the night watch. She hoped they'd fallen asleep tonight. With the moon behind a cotton cloud, she couldn't see anyone patrolling the main decks. And her vision wasn't strong enough to discern any movement in the crow's nest.

Emily exhaled a deep breath and climbed out, keeping herself low as she crossed to the mainmast. She ducked between the longboats and listened. Near-calm waters softly lapped against the hull and nothing more, not a snore, nor a footstep. She crossed the open space and reached the door to the navigation room, once again waiting, watching. Emily scanned the area for witnesses, and her heart punched into her throat as she turned the knob slowly to avoid squeaks. It opened enough for her to slip inside.

The room was dark, and Emily wanted to use her cell phone for the flashlight feature, but that would be stupid. Her hands slipped along the wall, stopping when she reached the door to the captain's quarters. Emily pressed an ear on the battered surface, but no sounds came from the other side.

Emily placed her hand on the final knob.

If she went inside, she would be violating Captain Lemoine's personal space, and whatever grain of trust she'd earned would blow away in the breeze, never to be recovered. The captain had driven home how important trust was on this ship, and after the crew threatened him, did he have anyone he could trust?

Emily didn't want to hurt anyone. But she had friends, a simple job, a cute apartment, and a plant. What she'd considered a fairly successful life, ignoring the fact that she was broke and the most important men in her life had betrayed her. It was what she knew. Emily was confident in her world and her choices. She could be who she was. Here she had to hide, pretend, deceive. It was exhausting, and she couldn't wait to get home.

Emily had to find her necklace and put it on. Failure was not an option, because no number of favors from the captain would save her from the articles she'd signed.

Exhaling a deep breath, she turned the knob.

EMILY CLOSED HERSELF IN the cabin with only a tiny dot of a flame at the bottom of a melted candle. Blood swished in her ears, and her heart pounded in her chest. She exhaled deep breaths to slow it down. She needed to hear. Focusing herself, she listened for a stirring or footsteps. Coughs or snores. Creaks of wood underfoot or a gasp of surprise.

All she could pick up were the soft sounds of deep slumber. She jutted her arms around to prevent herself from smacking into anything and causing a disruptive noise, but only a few steps in, her knee knocked the captain's bed post. Emily strained to bite back a grunt of pain just as moonlight broke free and filtered in through the row of windows. She frowned, keeping her swears at Mother Nature to herself and took advantage of the light provided.

The extravagant interior stole her breath. Underfoot was a woven rug. His bed was small, perhaps full size, with curving shapes carved into the frame. Numerous shelves and cabinets lined the room. He clearly liked to read. Then again, with no electronics, what else would a person do?

The captain's desk was solid wood with a quill and inkpot next to an hourglass. Curiosity pulled her toward it, and an open book sat on the surface. She tried to read the antique cursive, but a combination of the lighting and archaic language left Emily following the beautiful curves without understanding anything but dates and times.

Emily moved toward the book, many of which appeared to be older captain's logs—details of everything the captain had done, had taken, and had explored. Nothing would be more exciting to read, but her time was limited.

The captain shifted in bed, and Emily froze, focusing on the pattern of breaths and seeking changes. He was still asleep. He may have been used to sleeping through noise and movement, but she couldn't take any chances. Where would the captain keep a valuable necklace?

Emily tapped her chin and turned, reassessing everything over again. In front of the desk, the captain's jerkin was draped over a chairback. Emily tiptoed across the room, keeping the creaks to a minimum.

The captain turned over in bed, a startling rustle, and Emily gasped and slapped a hand over her mouth. The swishing returned to her ears, and Emily found to calm herself. Seconds stretched and her breathing strained, Emily released the spent air from her burning lungs and listened. He was still asleep.

Emily closed the distance and patted the fabric, seeking the telltale lump of her amethyst pendant. She heard a metallic jostle, and she gasped with excitement. It was here! Emily scrambled to find the pocket.

"You there! Halt!" a scratchy voice said from the door.

A lantern shined from behind her, and in desperation, Emily's trembling fingers moved faster. She was too close to give up now. She couldn't get caught. Breaths pumped in and out of her chest. More and more, she scrambled, metal jingling. Emily gripped the material and scraped at it with her nails, trying to find an opening to reach the gem.

"I said halt!" Loud boot steps pounded on the floor, closing the distance rapidly. "Captain!"

Shuffling and clattering came from the bed.

Faster, faster. She needed to pull the amethyst over her head, and this would all be over. There, an opening. Emily squeezed a hand inside, and her fingertips brushed against cold metal. A powerful fist gripped her wrist, locking her movements in place. She fought him. She had to fight. The consequences were too much to bear. Tears pressed against her eyes. She couldn't give up, but the night watchman was too strong. Picturing for a flash, all the men with their hungry grins prowling toward her, Emily sniffled. How could she have failed? She was so careful.

"Captain!" the night watchman repeated, squeezing harder. Bedding flung aside, and the captain sat upright, eyes meeting the man holding her. "I saw the bootless bugger sneaking inside, and I came at once."

Emily knew little of the era's slang, but that descriptor couldn't be nice. She faced her captor. The bearded waif of a man with a yellow glowing face from the lantern stared her down, refusing to release her.

The captain stood from his bed, tugging up his baggy breeches. Emily exhaled a deep, shaky breath while giving him the once over. His chest was broad, taut, and streaked with short dark hair like dabbled brush strokes. Without them fastened, his breeches slipped low, showing off sculpted hips. And Emily wanted nothing more at that moment than to run her hands over his body and feel the movement of his muscles under her touch. She wanted his thick arms to wrap around her body and pull her close. He was painfully handsome. Looking at him truthfully hurt, because she could never have a man like that. The minute she decided she wanted him, the timer on a betrayal began, and Emily couldn't survive another.

"Why the urgency, Hyde? Is something of concern with Porter here?" Emily noticed his use of her last name. He was still upset with her. But rather than speak directly to his guard, Captain Lemoine looked at Emily, and his face wasn't friendly. A sinking feeling in her chest told her that grain of trust had blown away.

Chapter 10

AT CAPTAIN ERIC LEMOINE'S question, the night watchman released his grip on Emile. There was nowhere for the man to go anyhow, and Lemoine didn't want anyone's hands on Emile but his own. He expected, with Emile's lengthy study of the articles, he understood section two. Robbery between two men aboard resulted in the guilty having his ears and nose slit before abandonment on a harsh shore. Emile Porter would risk mutilation and desertion for a necklace? It must've been far more valuable than he'd imagined, and he was right to keep it on his person. But had Lemoine been sitting on a vast treasure all this while? Could this simple jewel solve all his problems?

And the puzzle grew.

"He...he smiled, sir," Hyde said nervously.

Once again, Lemoine had to cover for the strange man who didn't understand their seafaring ways. The last thing he needed was more trouble for Emile—which meant, for himself.

"Smiling is cause for disruption to my sleep?" Lemoine crossed his arms over his bare chest to flex his thick biceps. He'd certainly noticed Emile's not-so-subtle gaze, and Lemoine like it.

"I thought he was a larcener, sir. Or he meant you harm." Hyde's confidence slipped.

"No one is a threat to anyone else on this ship. Must I remind you to keep your eyes on the sea?" Lemoine kept his tone firm, but he wasn't upset. Hyde had prevented Emile from retrieving the necklace. Since Lemoine, too, withheld its value from the crew, he was just as guilty of defrauding the company of its fair share. "You are dismissed."

Hyde took one last look at Emile before following orders. There was a flicker of suspicion there. Keeping Emile safe was growing more difficult by the day. When the door closed, the captain was left alone with Emile, bathed only in faded moonlight.

Lemoine released his flex and approached his newest recruit. "Larceny is a severe offense."

"I didn't steal anything from anyone."

"Then how did you come into possession of that necklace you're so desperate to retrieve?"

A fury pinched Emile's gentle face. "Are you accusing me of stealing from Captain Sinclair?"

"Tell me the truth." All he wanted was answers.

The fascinating man shifted his gaze aside at the question. What was he hiding? The secrets and unanswered questions drove Lemoine mad! Captain Lemoine moved, his body so close to Emile's he could feel the heat radiating off him. The smell of flowers had faded away, but there was something else. Something deeper, more luxurious, even more puzzling.

"I can't." Emile met his gaze, sure of his answer. "I can't tell you. You wouldn't believe me, anyway."

It was an answer, just not one Lemoine wanted, and it satisfied nothing. He searched the dashing man's smooth face, as if he could find the answers buried behind those hazel eyes or resting on those soft, curving lips. The longer he lingered, the more Emile's breathing picked up. This fascinating stranger wanted him just as much. If only it weren't forbidden! His lips were so close. One little touch wouldn't be discovered.

But Lemoine couldn't stop at one, and he couldn't stay quiet enough, either. Giving in to temptation would lead them both down a path of ruin. Lemoine couldn't do it. He was too close to having what he needed, and he couldn't further endanger Emile.

The beautiful man was proficient at that on his own.

Finally, Lemoine identified the scent, and he lifted his brows. "Chocolate."

Emile laughed, and he covered his forehead with his hand, blocking his beautiful eyes from Lemoine's view. Shoulders shook from peals of laughter.

"I hardly understand what could cause such amusement." For a moment, he worried Emile was laughing at his reaction to the man.

Emile opened the leather pouch on his belt. A rustle of paper followed in the darkness. "Open your mouth," he whispered.

Oh, how he yearned to! But Lemoine couldn't. He had to fight these clear signs Emile wanted him to. It had to be enough. The mutual attraction alone had to satisfy until they landed at port. "I cannot."

Emile laughed. "Is chocolate forbidden on this ship? I didn't see it specified in the articles."

"Rarely is anything ever just chocolate." The captain closed his eyes, wishing Emile would open up to him. They may not have physical relations, but they could be friends, and Lemoine wanted that connection. He wanted to trust someone. He felt like Emile was that someone, but the handsome stranger refused at every turn.

"Well, this is, and it's melting in my fingers. Just take it. No strings attached."

Lemoine looked at the soft hand. A small square of chocolate was pinched between his fingers. Could he have one taste? Could he stop at one?

EMILY HAD TO STOP herself from laughing at the absurdity. The captain acted like a piece of chocolate was devilry sent to trick him into burning in hell. But the longer he delayed, the longer she got to memorize his naked torso, and did she ever enjoy the view. She was so close, the smallest wave could tilt the hull in her favor, and she could reach out and grab him for balance.

A girl could only hope.

The captain still hesitated. It was a risk to offer a modern treat, but she could explain that away. "It's not stolen. It's mine. I brought it along, and I'm offering it to you."

The captain closed his eyes. "I insist I cannot."

So damned strange. Emily popped the chocolate into her mouth and licked her fingers clean. She appreciated the flavor after the tasteless crunchy biscuit she'd dined on. The captain was into her. That much was obvious. Under different circumstances, she wouldn't turn him down, either. But this wasn't the twenty-first century, and these weren't her rules. The moment he discovered what lied beneath her handcrafted clothing, he'd kill her—regardless of whether he'd want to. The betrayal would destroy him, and the articles were clear.

"I know I don't belong here, and I know I've caused you a great deal of trouble. For what it's worth, I'm sorry. If you'll return my necklace, I'll be on my way."

The captain opened his eyes, gazing at her with a trickle of anger. "The articles you signed clearly describe all prizes are to be divided per the shares agreement. That means the necklace belongs to the crew now. At Nassau, I will have the appraiser document its value, and I'll sell it. Each man will get his due."

Emily refrained from jutting a finger at his bare chest. "That necklace is not from Sinclair's ship. It's not part of the prize. It's my personal belonging and, according to section two of the articles, your withholding of my personal belonging is robbing me."

The captain's lips twitched, as if he were fighting back a grin of amusement. Emily hated when he did that—treating her arguments as invalid. She wasn't stupid. She signed carefully.

Soft yellows and oranges of dawn stretched along the smooth horizon through the cabin windows. It was a breathtaking sight of beauty she never could have imagined. A sudden and stupid urge had her reaching for her pouch again to take a photo with her cell phone camera, but she quickly reminded herself that would mean death. She smoothed her sweaty palms against her breeches.

"It's a beautiful sight, isn't it?"

"I didn't think anything could top the night sky."

"Tell me," the captain whispered. "If I were to return the necklace to your possession, where would you go?"

Emily gazed back at the horizon. "Home."

"And where is such a place?"

The captain was always fishing for information. Was she that weird? "Far from here."

"As I suspected," he said with a tinge of disappointment. But he wasn't wrong to realize Emily didn't belong. Wisconsin was a long way off from the Caribbean Sea of 1715.

"Then why do you keep asking?" She turned on him, curious herself why she, of all the newest members of the crew, kept getting singled out for questioning.

The captain studied her as the dawn light shined in her face. "Because I'm struck by a fatal case of curiosity, but I'm grateful you continue to reject me."

Emily blinked. He hounded her for answers, but appreciated she didn't give them. Now, who was the strange one? Emily could tell where she wasn't wanted. Emily turned and strolled toward the cabin door. If she left, he'd be turning her back on the necklace. Glancing over her shoulder, she said, "I've already told you. Return my necklace, and I'll cause you no more trouble."

The captain didn't move. Not a word passed between his lips. Emily walked out.

EMILY LEANED AGAINST THE port rail, watching the morning light dance on the surface of the sea, wishing for coffee. Sailors around her manned their positions. She didn't have one, and no one assigned her to anything, so she absorbed the breathtaking view and tampered down the guilt creeping in. She wasn't a freeloader, but she didn't know the first thing about sailing. She wished she did, if only to take her mind off the captain and give her hands something to do.

Captain Lemoine didn't want her, but he wouldn't let her go, either, and Emily couldn't figure out why. If he would've given her the necklace, she would've been home by now, laughing with Angela at the absurdity of this adventure. And telling Robin she was lucky to have avoided it entirely.

But she also knew Captain Lemoine would haunt her dreams.

"Porter!" a stern man's voice commanded behind her, and it wasn't the captain's.

Emily turned, stomach clenching, and found the quartermaster with a clipboard in hand and a frown on his brow. "I assigned you hammock seventy-two, correct?"

Emily had snuck out of bed to slip into the captain's cabin with no intention of returning to her hammock tonight. Since she was trying to be stealthy, she hadn't packed it up at that hour. She'd since forgotten.

Without waiting for her excuse, Quartermaster Price continued, "Leaving hammocks hanging on the gun deck impedes movement in the event of an attack. Secure your bedding in the net over the rail."

Since he was the man in charge of her still-yet unknown punishment, Emily thought it wise to be kind. "I'm sorry. It won't happen again."

Quartermaster Price nodded, and Emily rushed below deck to correct her oversight. She found her lone hammock swaying with the ship's movement, but she couldn't reach the hooks attaching it to the ceiling. Searching around, she found a wood crate and moved it over. Emily stepped up and worked the fastenings, freeing her hammock. Wiping the sweat from her brow, a man cleared his throat.

Now what?

Emily spun and lost her balance with the heavy sack in her arms and a sway of the ship. The rotund man with a grease all over his apron caught her and gently set her on her feet. He wore a friendly smile. "I'm Giles, the cook. We haven't met formally, but since I didn't see you at breakfast, I thought I'd bring you sustenance." He held out a biscuit, and Emily accepted it. "You're not a sailor, I'd wager."

"No, not at all." Emily bit off a dry bite, but since she was hungry, she wasn't complaining.

Giles beamed. "I expected as much. Well, a piece of advice for you. Tend to your duties and keep to yourself. Some of these men are not friendly to new faces."

"And you're not one of them."

Giles winked.

"Thanks you for the tip." Emily swallowed down her biscuit, throat dry like a Wisconsin wintry morning. The ship's stale air didn't help, and with the sweat beading on her body and the salty, sticky air, Emily would welcome snow.

Giles offered her a cup of mystery liquid, and Emily downed it without a second thought.

"Good luck to you." Giles took the cup back from her and climbed down to the galley. In a sea of seventy or more men, she had two friends she could count on. Emily lugged her heavy pack up the ladder and leaned it against the rail. After sticking her head over the edge, she found the netting Price had mentioned. With a great struggle, she forced the pack into position neatly along the row of others. Emily panted with exhaustion, tired from a brief night's sleep.

A loud yawn came from behind her, and Emily stood upright and turned, ready to defend herself against further scrutiny. But Fergus's friendly face relaxed her.

"Yer hammock was empty half th'night."

"Couldn't sleep."

Fergus leaned against the rail next to her elbow, and Emily copied his posture, both staring off at the rising dawn. "Any family awaiting ye?" he asked.

"Do I have kids of my own?" she clarified. "No, but I have a houseplant and an ex…" Emily trailed off. She could give Fergus some truth, but spun for her safety. "A woman I courted recently, but I lost her." Emily hoped wherever Angela was, she was safe and happy.

Fergus lightheartedly patted Emily's shoulder. "Yer Angela? It's a man's veritable nightmare."

Loud footsteps captured Emily's attention. She turned to find the captain, and his intense gaze met hers. He'd dressed fully in a cocked hat, breeches up where they belonged, and a tunic under his long coat. He looked hot as hell, but she preferred the half naked version. "We land in Nassau in three days hence."

The crew cheered at the captain's announcement, and, eager to reach port, the men suddenly had more bounce in their steps. The masts swiveled in harmony, and a breeze caught the sails with a sharp snap. Emily grinned at the beauty of it. She watched, enamored, as the boatswain hollered commands to help the men coordinate their movements with chants. The helmsman, who wasn't the captain, took to the wheel and turned the rudder. The force pushed Emily against the rail, and her cheeks hurt from smiling so hard.

"Ye hear that?" Fergus said, voice bubbling with excitement. "Three days! Th'captain shall retain his command long enough fur us tae depart this wretched vessel, thanks tae ye."

Wretched vessel sounded accurate to her. She watched the captain on the quarterdeck, shoulders squared, hands clasped behind his back, and chin lifted as he gazed at the horizon. She'd never left the country, so a chance to visit a historical site on a tropical island sounded very appealing. Even better if she could shower and find real food. "I'm looking forward to exploring."

Fergus lit up. "Join me. I know of some exciting places."

Emily wanted a day of debauchery on shore with the captain, but she'd rather have Fergus than no one. "I can do that, sure."

Fergus grinned. "Time tae get tae work. Ye signed and now ye're expected tae sail this ship," Fergus said. "Since I canny wait tae disembark, I'll assist. Are ye coming along, then?"

Emily rubbed her forearm sheepishly. "I don't know how to sail."

Fergus smiled and patted her shoulder. "I thought no', but ye must learn sometime, pirate. Come along."

Emily followed her friend and smiled at his back, happy he was understanding rather than judgmental. As they crossed amidships, she glanced up at the captain next to the helmsman. He looked like a leader, strong, brave, and sexy as hell. She wanted him to notice not only was she cooperating, but she also wasn't attempting to break into his cabin again. Mostly, she just wanted him to notice her.

Emily's research left her dreaming of what life was like beyond the worn documents—how the men experienced all the wonders of the sea's power. And now here she was—an actual pirate, signed articles and all. But if she had to do any real pirating, Emily just knew she'd be the worst, because Emily wasn't a thief, and she didn't hurt people. The closest thing to a weapon she'd touched was a replica sword hanging in her bedroom.

Captain Lemoine's eyes followed her.

11

Chapter 11

NOT MUCH TIME PASSED before the glitz and glamour of living on a ship had waned. When Emily was young, her mother couldn't afford lavish trips. Instead, they went camping in the upper peninsula of Michigan—only a few hours' drive from home—with her mother's friends and their children. Emily's favorite site was Wells State Park on Lake Michigan. It had a beautiful beige sandy beach, fresh water for swimming, and hiking trails through the woods—an adventure so close to home.

And in the evenings, they'd roast marshmallows over an open firepit. When Emily was in her teen years, she was allowed to drink beer with the adults. And when she was an adult herself, she continued the tradition with her friends. She, Angela, and Robin swapped scandalous stories from their community college years. The three of them would lounge on the beach at sunrise, watching the pinks and purples dance in the sky and the sun shimmering on the lake's surface. Loons sang their eerie yodel.

At the end of each trip, she'd be exhausted, dirty, and sore from an air mattress, wishing for a hot meal. A short drive would get her all the modern luxuries she needed, including a hot shower.

This was so much worse than camping.

The physically demanding shifts in the salty sea air and penetrating sun left her needing a nap. One more day of this and she'd beg for rat duty below deck, except Emily didn't have the heart to kill the little dudes. They just wanted food and shelter like everyone else.

Emily pulled the line while Fergus expertly tied it, and Emily swiped a dirty arm across her sweaty brow and frowned. Because of a nightly chorus of snoring and thoughts of the captain on replay, Emily hadn't slept well. A poor diet of watered-down wine and stale crunchy biscuit, which resembled bread that had been left to harden in the sun for weeks, didn't help any. She'd known a pirate's diet was less than ideal, since scurvy and dysentery were major problems. All she could do was daydream about a cheeseburger and fries. A sizzle of grease from her favorite eatery filled her ears, and Emily turned her head to see if she had, in fact, lost her mind. They'd reach Nassau soon, but she wouldn't find a cheeseburger there.

With each passing hour, the quartermaster still hadn't called upon her for punishment. Emily began to believe it wouldn't happen. Maybe all those threats, all that excessive punishment in writing, had just been to scare people. No one really cut off someone's ears and nose for stealing, and no one really dropped someone off on a deserted island to die of thirst and exposure. The reality was, they were nice people—dirty, starved, and a little perverted—but nice in general.

"Porter, come with me," a familiar voice said behind her. The quartermaster had arrived.

Emily swallowed a thick lump, but it was caught in her dry throat.

Fergus wove the line around a belaying pin and stood straight beside her, as if he wanted to challenge Price for her attention. The quartermaster gestured with his head for her to follow. Emily met Fergus's concerned face, but he said nothing, only watched as she tilted her chin up, and walked off to whatever fate the quartermaster had in mind.

Below the main deck, in the aft of the gun deck, was Price's office, filled with rows and rows of old leather-bound books. These were not captain's logs. Of all the things she'd expected in a pirate's office—gold and jewels, namely—pleasure books were not it, since literacy rates were so low. The more she learned of the real pirates behind the legendary stories, the more she was intrigued. They weren't savage animals. They weren't greedy monsters slaughtering people for money. Pirates were just people, a product of their time and harsh circumstance. As much as she missed her modern amenities and well-rounded diet, this wasn't such a bad life.

Price closed the door on the two of them and sat behind his desk. He invited her to take a chair across from him, and Emily did. The quartermaster always held a seriousness to him, like someone who didn't know how to have fun. Perhaps he was allergic to it, but right now, he looked downright disgusted. That didn't bode well for Emily. "Do you know why I requested a meeting?"

"Is this about the rum?" It concerned her greatly that he'd needed days to settle this issue.

"Clearly, you're new to the world of free men. And you mustn't have been a merchant sailor at all. We have an understanding, a rank, that shall not be broken, no matter the issue at hand."

"I—" Emily tried to defend herself, but she gassed out. What excuse could she give that would satisfy him?

Price leaned forward, brow darkening. "Taking what isn't yours is stealing, no matter how noble the cause."

"But I'm one of the crew. The first section of the articles states all men have an equal claim to the provision and liquors and may use them at pleasure. I can't steal from myself."

Price's lips thinned. "Unless a scarcity makes it necessary to vote on the decision, but Lemoine convinced the men that wasn't needed."

Emily sat back. She had no right to freely give what wasn't hers to give, even if it solved the problem at the time. She'd jumped the proverbial gun to save an ass that didn't need saving.

"And even worse, you made a liar out of me." The anger festered, shifting the muscle in his jaw and twitching his eyelid.

"I didn't mean to undermine your authority. I was only trying to help the captain. They were so angry with him. I'm sorry." She hoped a sincere apology would be enough.

"The crew would agree with you, but there's a reason they aren't in charge. Both Lemoine and I have a right to settle a quarrel with you, which would take place on shore with swords and pistols. But after your embarrassing display out there, I'm of the esteem you know nothing of either weapons."

Price and the captain wanted to kill her? Emily couldn't even believe it. They *were* animals—filthy, disgusting, soulless monsters. "Well, you're right. I don't, so I guess it'll be an easy kill for you. Not so satisfying though, right?"

Emily was pissed, but she didn't have the guts to stand up and march out of there. Something about how he paused led her to believe there was more, perhaps a lesser sentence. So she waited.

Price glared. The anger remained. "Lemoine declined to punish you, but since we have to follow the articles to keep authority, trust, and order in place, I'm not."

A string of swears poured through Emily's mind, but she kept her mouth shut. When the quartermaster deposited her on Nassau for their duel, she'd run like hell. She had a feeling Fergus wouldn't turn her in. He'd go with her.

"To spare your life, I'm sentencing you to ten lashes."

Hearing what was to come drained her anger away, and the fear of exposure returned once again. Instead of facing a dozen or so starved merchant sailors, now there were several dozen pirates. "How exactly do you go about giving those lashes?"

Price squinted at her. "Our lashes are doled the same as any other. We found you tied to the mast on the verge of the same punishment, so I don't understand where the confusion stems from. Regardless, your sentencing will commence momentarily. Refrain from defying orders in the future."

Emily's eyes widened, and she nodded, not knowing what to say without angering him further. Getting the hint he was finished, she launched out of his office in a state of imbalance and terror like a chain shot from a cannon.

There was no pirate ship to rescue her from the pirates.

QUARTERMASTER PRICE HAD STATED his case. The man was right in his decision, but Captain Eric Lemoine couldn't do it. He couldn't choose to duel the beautiful young man and take his life, but he also understood a punishment had to happen for the crew to maintain its order.

Lemoine could never have done the quartermaster's job. He couldn't take a life or make anyone suffer.

Captain Donald Sinclair had been the one exception.

Price had scheduled Emile Porter's punishment for nine bells. While Captain Lemoine braided his hair, a flurry of activity had already begun on the deck—barrels moved out of the way, lines pushed aside. Price needed enough distance to apply the proper force.

Lemoine shucked his coat and folded it before resting it over his chairback. He removed his tunic and draped it carefully over the coat. He exhaled a few deep breaths. Ready to fulfill his promise, he squared his shoulders and marched out of his cabin.

All but the essential crew surrounded the mainmast. Price was speaking to the men, holding a modified rope—their cat-o'-nine-tails. Rope stung a little less than leather at first, but it took longer to heal. The rough surface and frayed ends left several more scrapes and burns than sharp leather did.

The men parted for him to pass, and most of them didn't object.

How strange. Lemoine snorted softly to himself.

He entered the circle and faced his crew, meeting them eye to eye. He nodded once to acknowledge their thoughts and his decision, and Lemoine faced the mast. Karl Dillon, their boatswain, did the honors of tying Lemoine to the mast, exposing his back to Price. Karl was an honorable man. He might appear round, but he was sharp as a knife. He kept this ship functional, kept the wind in the sails, and kept the men flowing as one.

Karl offered Lemoine a knotted fabric bite block. "Take this. It helps."

Without a word, Lemoine opened his mouth, and Karl inserted it just right. Lemoine bit down, the sun making him sweat, but the breeze helped keep him cool. The ties at his wrists were to help keep him steady. After all, he'd volunteered, and he wasn't afraid. He'd experienced the cat before, had the scars to prove it. It wasn't pleasant, but he'd be fine...eventually.

When he was a boy, on the verge of adulthood, he'd been in this same position. Back then, he'd been terrified. He didn't know how much it would hurt, and the grim faces around him scared him worse. Those adults were afraid for him. But now he was grown, a man experienced with the harsh realities of his lifestyle. One thing never changed: Lemoine kept his word.

Karl patted Lemoine's back in solidarity and stepped away.

A man broke from the crowd and rushed to his side. It was Emile, and Lemoine didn't want to face him. He knew the man would object, and Lemoine wasn't changing his mind.

Emile whispered in urgent tones, "What's going on? What are you doing?"

Lemoine couldn't answer. Emile figured it out and tugged at his bite block.

Lemoine didn't let go. There was nothing he could say that would appease the beautiful man. And causing a scene when this punishment should've been his would only add to the crew's disgruntlement.

They appreciated Emile giving them their rum.

They hated Lemoine for allowing it and taking it away.

They hated Price for lying about it.

This had to happen, just as it was.

But as expected, Emile wouldn't give up. "Talk to me, please."

Price continued to answer questions from the crowd. The quartermaster was allowing Emile to get his answers, so on the next tug, Lemoine relaxed his grip on the bite block.

"Why are you tied up?" Emile whispered in a panic. "You didn't do anything wrong. Is this the mutiny?"

Captain Lemoine turned his head to meet those hazel eyes, now filled with fear. "I owed you a favor. Consider it repaid."

"Repaid? Are you saying...?" Tears glistened on Emile's lids. "No, you can't. This isn't right. I screwed up. It's my fault. Not yours. Please, don't do this, please."

Lemoine hadn't seen such guilt in a long time, but doing this would placate the crew and keep Lemoine's word honorable. Mostly, his choice kept Emile from facing this pain, because Lemoine couldn't handle if the roles were reversed. "Return my bite block," he said and opened his mouth.

Emile wiped his nose on the back of his hand and shoved the block forcibly into his mouth. "You're a selfish ass."

Emile ran off into the crowd, and Lemoine's brows lifted as he adjusted the bite block's position. Why would Emile assume such colorful things about him for this selfless act? With the cat about to hit, Lemoine couldn't let his thoughts wander. He focused on breathing deeply.

Price appeared and touched his shoulder. "Are we ready?"

Lemoine mumbled, and Price removed the block. "Push my braid aside." He held his mouth open again, and Price returned the block and swept his braid off his back.

The quartermaster lifted the whip. "And we begin."

The whip hit a second before each count, preventing Lemoine from tensing before the strike. Price wasn't going gently on the whip. Sometimes Lemoine wondered about him. Strike after strike lashed his bare skin. Blood ran down to his breeches. Each cut was like a hot knife searing through skin, and it burned, but for Emile's sake, he kept his face as blank as he could.

But he met the man's worried gaze.

Lemoine wanted to show him ten lashes were nothing. He didn't want the man to worry more. Emile was already on the verge of hysterics, such an uncommon thing for a man his age, but that only added to the mysterious puzzle. Where would someone find a man so beautiful with such strange mannerisms and clothing? Focusing on Emile lessened the pain, but by the final few strikes, Lemoine's face showed the burning agony.

"Ten."

Lemoine bit the block and pinched his face, trying to keep his eyes on Emile, but this last one, he couldn't. The whip came down hard, and Lemoine held his breath. The searing heat tore through damaged flesh, and more blood poured down his fiery flesh.

But it was over.

Lemoine dropped the bite block and panted. While Karl untied his wrists, Price coiled his cat. His face showed sorrow and regret, but Lemoine knew, deep down, Price had wanted to do that for a while. He'd jest with him later.

Lemoine cast Emile a comforting look before trying to stand and failing.

"DOCTOR!" A MAN SHOUTED.

Emily's instincts were to run to his side. This was a medical emergency, and she was equipped to respond, but the captain's gaze told her not to. It would be too suspicious for her to attend to the needs of the man who'd already taken her punishment for her. And damn him for it. She was so angry he'd hurt himself for her sake.

But he saved her life.

Just as she'd saved his.

They were even, but that didn't stop her from wanting to help him. She couldn't imagine the indescribable pain, and he'd held himself together, stoic, brave, taking the licks without a cry of pain. It wasn't the first time. Captain Lemoine's muscular, broad back was crisscrossed with raised scars—previous whippings.

Emily would've been screaming and pleading for mercy—if they'd decided to go forward with the cat after they stripped her top naked. She still would've screamed and pleaded for mercy.

A stout man with a long white beard pushed through the crew and assessed the captain's wounds. At least there was a real doctor on the ship. Emily's relief was palpable.

"Take 'em down to the infirmary." The heavy medic climbed down the ladder ahead of his patient, and in moments, the injured captain was assisted down into the bowels of the ship.

No one had ever sacrificed themselves for her like that, favor owed or not, and Emily didn't know what to do with that. She wished she could be in the infirmary with him. Taking the lashes was the deal he'd made without her consent, but healing from the wounds was something else.

The crew mumbled to each other, and Boatswain Karl commanded everyone to return to their stations. Emily struggled through the day, doing whatever Fergus directed her to do, planning how she could help the stubborn captain.

Chapter 12

EMILY HAD SPENT THAT night tossing and turning in her hammock, covering her ears against the barrage of snores, creaks, and night shift orders. All she could think about was the agony the captain must've been suffering on her account. She wished she could sneak into his cabin and tend his wounds. It was the least she could do, but that was too risky. Even a wind of favoritism would be enough for the crew to uphold the last of the articles: *no boy or woman to be allowed amongst them.* They didn't need to prove any bedtime activities to punish her with death. The assumption was enough. Emily wasn't going to risk her life just to scold the captain, and she wasn't going to send away a perfectly qualified doctor from his duty.

All day, the crew hadn't gossiped one peep about the captain's punishment. Price had answered all their questions to their satisfaction, and that was that. Unlike them, Emily couldn't forget it, but she didn't know what to do about it.

Emily finished tying her line and rose to take a break and stretch her back. Her eyes immediately moved to the navigation room, through which the captain's cabin rested. And as if her wishes simply came true, Captain Lemoine emerged. He wasn't wearing his coat, just breeches and a tunic. But he was alive, and a flush of relief eased the ache in her bones. That was the only news she'd received on his condition since the whipping. He was alive.

Captain Lemoine moved with the stiffness of fresh wounds, climbing up the quarterdeck, steady on his feet, and he spoke with the helmsman, Hodgens. Emily had a small chat with the man the other day. He had the personality of bread—ordinary, bland, but with a little warming up, delightful. They were too far away for Emily to hear them.

"Sails!" the man in the crow's nest shouted.

Their heads turned, and Emily copied them. She skimmed the horizon, but seeing nothing discernible with the naked eye, she watched a man rush below deck and quickly retrieve the quartermaster. Price joined the captain and Hodgens on the quarterdeck, and both Price and Lemoine took turns observing from the spyglass. Neither of them looked pleased. Before she realized what she was doing, Emily's feet brought her within earshot of the men just as Boatswain Karl joined them. Master gunner, McKee, followed, but she hadn't met him, only caught his name in passing.

"Royal Navy," Captain Lemoine said with a grim set to his jaw.

"Are you certain?" Price asked with a shocking tremble in his voice. Emily hadn't believed the man capable of feeling anything but grumpiness.

Captain Lemoine returned the spyglass to his eye and flinched. Emily assumed it was from soreness, not worry. His voice was light, almost joyful, just like when she's first met him. "Three gun decks, English flag. Perhaps I'm mistaken?" Emily smiled. The captain was back to his old self.

Then she processed the words. That size ship could be nothing but a man-o'-war.

Price accepted the offered spyglass and peered through it. The crew, without critical tasks, filled in around her, awaiting news and orders, and Fergus appeared at her shoulder. She noticed the lithe man frequently stayed by her side; this time he was grinning like a fool.

"What part of a man-o'-war makes you happy?" Emily asked.

"I, fur one, am grateful tae have skipped signing th'articles. When we're caught, I'll be spared th'noose."

Emily frowned. "And you don't care that I won't be?"

Fergus looked at her with a softness she hadn't expected. "I dae care, but if ye'd heeded ma advice, ye wouldn't be worried noo. Th'three o' us, who refrained, shall be free, ainlie noo we dinny have tae wait fur Nassau."

Emily's voice grew louder. "Do you hear yourself? Have you ever considered no one deserves the noose?"

Heads turned to her while waiting for the captain's news and orders.

Fergus raked a hand through his red, bushy hair and caught glances of the crew around him. His voice quieted, "Aye. I dae." He gazed at her as if the words were meant for Emily only. "If ye swear ye were pressed, th'Crown shall be lenient. Extra steps fur ye, since ye signed, but still th'same outcome."

Emily folded her arms over her chest, not satisfied with his confidence. "You think if I lie in court, they'll free me? Have you read the hist—?" Emily cut herself off before earning herself more questions. Many pirates claimed to be pressed for the sole purpose of not being sentenced. It didn't work much of the time.

"When th'*Sea Lion* is captured, consider ma advice this time?"

"Your advice was not to sign because these people are worse than Sinclair, but you're clearly wrong."

Fergus flustered. "I'm noo wrong about them." He nodded toward the ship approaching.

She wasn't going to give him the satisfaction of an answer to that. If the Royal Navy arrested her, she was as good as dead, like all the others. The Royal Navy didn't conscript pirates into their ranks, so the only other option was to flee their custody. But since they were surrounded by ocean and sharks, there was nowhere to flee toward.

Emily focused on the captain. He was their leader. He knew what to do. The quartermaster returned the spyglass to the captain, and Boatswain Karl asked, "Your orders, captain?"

Captain Lemoine kept his eye on the man-o'-war. The grim set to his jaw returned. "The barque can outpace her if we dump the cargo."

Because of their size and heavy artillery, and carrying hundreds of trained soldiers, man-o'-war ships were cumbersome, gliding castles. If the *Sea Lion* was within the warship's range, the damage would be fast, efficient, and catastrophic. If instead the soldiers boarded the *Sea Lion*, the discrepancy in the number of soldiers versus pirates meant a slaughter was inevitable. She glanced at all the worried faces around her. None of them deserved to die like that. They had to dump the cargo, but Emily expected no pirate wanted to give up their loot in an escape attempt when they weren't certain about being caught. How else was everyone going to be fed, paid, and remain complacent?

"Naught else can be done?" Price asked, paling in fear.

"The *Sea Lion* is a formidable foe against merchant ships. And I'd wager friendly competition against a sixth-rate frigate, but I commandeered her for speed, not her guns. If we fight a first-rate man-o'-war, we'll lose," Captain Lemoine said with finality.

Emily swallowed a thick lump. If they were only a day or so from Nassau. Hungry, unpaid, and desperate pirates should be content for one day. They wouldn't turn on the new recruits... They wouldn't discover things they shouldn't...

Those worries only mattered if they escaped the warship's chase.

The first cannon rang out across the surface, followed by a splash. Time was of the essence. The captain gave his instructions to Karl, and the bald boatswain dished out the orders to the men. The assigned crew flew up the rigging and ratlines, preparing for full speed ahead.

"Dump it," Price said with defeat. Emily didn't like that disappointment and edge to his tone, so her concerns over the crew were justified.

The captain gave out his next orders, and Boatswain Karl barked them to the next teams. "Jettison the hold!"

Men poured down the ladders to obey, and Karl turned to her and Fergus. "You two, bring up the sand." Karl brushed past them on his way to supervise the change of sails.

Emily cocked her head at Fergus for clarification.

"Follow me." Fergus moved down the levels below, and in a room opposite the hold, Fergus opened the door and hefted a pair of burlap bags over his shoulders. All the warmth drained from Emily's face. How was she going to carry those? "Can ye handle a bag?" Fergus gave her a sly smile.

The bags were probably heavier than the barrel of rum had been. A small nervous smile tilted her lips, and Fergus handed her one. Emily hugged it, straining, and her knees felt the weight.

"After th'first crew rushes up wi' th'stores, we'll make our way. Gaining speed right noo is more important than gripping th'deck."

Another cannon fired, and shortly thereafter, wood crunched on impact. Panicked shouts came from below deck, but Emily was so preoccupied with understanding her assignment, she didn't give any other thought to it. "What are we doing?"

"In battle, th'deck becomes mighty slippery. Sand gives a foothold."

Emily pictured clanging swords and gunshots ringing her eardrums. And since the waves weren't crashing over the rail, Fergus must've meant blood. Emily's stomach flipped. She inhaled several humid, musty breaths from the dank belly of the ship. When Fergus commanded, she rushed up behind him on the ladder, knees screaming with each step.

Other pirates were already shouting for them to move out of the way by the time they reached the main deck.

Fergus tore into his bag and sprinkled it around like ice melt on a Wisconsin sidewalk. Finally, something familiar.

Emily couldn't tear hers. "Can I get a hand?"

Fergus smiled and ripped a hole in her bag. They both shook gritty sand all over the deck while some of it fell between the planks.

"I have a little brother back home." Fergus smiled wistfully. Emily figured he was picturing his impending escape. "He dreams o' sailing th'seas. I tried tae change his mind, but according tae his correspondence, th'lad is firm. Mum and Da insist oan encouraging him. I haven't th'heart tae wreck his dreams wi' th'reality o' merchant sea life. Are ye ever going tae tell me where ye came from? Ye and th'lost woman, Angela?

This time, the cannon blast got her attention. Emily straightened with her half-empty bag and followed the trajectory of the massive ball as it soared through the sky. It aimed right at the bulwark in front of her. She stared like a deer in the headlights, unable to make her limbs react, unable to believe what she was seeing.

At the last second, before the iron ball blasted through the bulwark right at Emily, she was forcibly shoved down for cover, head hitting the planks. The sandbag spilled, throwing a cloud in her face. Spots danced in her vision. Emily coughed. Her ears rang a high-pitched whistle above the crunching of wood and shouts from the crew.

When her vision cleared, she stared at the brilliant blue sky with white puffs of clouds floating on by like a gentle parade. She remembered one of her picnics with Angela while camping. They'd brought out a large blanket to cover the grass, and her friend carried a basket with junk food and beer. They'd crack and chug a few cans, and after the buzz eased every muscle in Emily's body, she'd drop over onto the blanket and gaze at the shapes in the clouds. The last time they'd partaken in the biannual excursion, Angela had pointed and said, "Over there. It's a rabbit!"

Emily had squinted. "I only see Wile E. Coyote chasing the Road Runner. Did you know his middle initial stands for Ethelbert?" Emily had chuckled at her own observation. "You're just too drunk to see straight. Toss me some Cheetos."

Angela had sat up too quickly. "Whoa, Road Runner's doing circles." They'd both broken out in laughter, and Angela tried twice to get her hand into the basket. "Too bad Robin had a shift today. Why didn't Tyler want to join?"

"He's starting on the business. It's pretty time consuming."

"Well, I'm excited for you. What are you selling or what service are you offering? I'll be your first customer." Angela tore into a fun size bag of Cheetos.

Emily considered. In all their conversations, that never came up. "I don't know."

Emily blinked. The ACME anvil floated overhead.

The ringing subsided and sweaty men's heads dipped in and out of her vision. Their thundering boots rattled the wood beneath her head. The wind had been knocked from her lungs. She sucked in a breath and sat up, rubbing the back of her head and coughing on the sand dust. Other than the smack on the skull and serious bruising that would hurt tomorrow, she was okay.

The bulwark was splintered and a big hole remained where it had stopped by for a visit. How did she avoid any serious damage? Someone must've pushed her out of the way on time.

The crew was focused on moving the ship away. Through the cannonball hole, the navy ship sank further into the distance. They were outrunning it! With a smile of relief on her face, Price stood on the quarterdeck shouting orders. Why wasn't Captain Lemoine up there? Emily craned her neck around but couldn't see him or her friend anywhere. She rose on wobbly legs and hooked her hand around the first man's arm, who came close enough, stopping him in his tracks. "Where's Fergus?"

He shrugged out of her grip and said, "Infirmary."

Emily's empty stomach twisted like she was going to be sick. "Which deck is he on?"

The meaty, broad-shouldered pirate pointed to the ladder. "Orlop. Two down, swing aft. When you see the coil of messenger cable, you're in the right place." He marched away without another word, and Emily made her way down and paused with a hand supporting her woozy head. Her damage might not have been from the cannonball, but the fall had been nasty.

After regaining her composure, she fumbled down the next ladder on unsure footing. She swung herself around the post and found the floor tilting. Emily paused and pulled in several deep breaths to steady herself. If Fergus had sacrificed himself for her, how would she ever forgive herself? Twice now men have risked their lives for her sake, and they didn't even know her!

Finding the door ajar and a serious commotion inside, Emily panted from exertion and worry while she peered inside. It was worse than she thought.

13

Chapter 13

THE SMELL OF BLOOD. The hurried and hushed voices. The groans of pain. All by the flicker of candle lanterns. Emily couldn't figure out what was happening. She pushed her way through the activity in the suffocating room. A beat-up old plank was settled over a pair of barrels, upon which a man writhed in pain. Fergus stood by his side, head tipped low.

Emily shuffled over to her friend, and a spin of her head had her gripping Fergus for balance. The redhead was startled at first, but he looked at her and smiled. "How are ye feeling? Ye took a good knock tae th'head. I dinny want tae leave ye up there, but ye weren't bleeding. We're waiting on Meeks. He'll see ye next. Sit over here while ye wait." Fergus moved a crate full of supplies and brushed the surface of the barrel clean with his hand.

"Meeks? Who's Meeks?" Emily asked, sitting and pressing a hand against her forehead.

"Th'doctor. Ye must be hurting." His gentle eyes searched her body for wounds.

Emily dropped her hand, fully expecting a headache. "I'll live. What happened? Are you okay?"

"I'm fine. Th'captain shoved me over an' tackled ye. If he hadn't, ye'd be oan this table, an' I'd be sitting in yer seat.

Emile." Fergus rested a hand on Emily's shoulder. "I dinny admit when I'm wrong much, because it disny happen often. The captain is a fine man. Yer instincts were right in signing."

Emily didn't sign because of the captain, but that wasn't worth spoiling his apology for. "Thanks, Fergus, but why the change of heart?"

A large muscle-bound man with a shiny dome on top of his head ducked into the small space. "Meeks is dead. The last shot hit him square in the middle."

"The doctor is dead?" Emily's pulse quickened with the emergency response she'd trained for. She stood and swayed on her unsteady feet.

Retail workers often tried to lift too much and pulled a muscle, or they dropped something on their foot, or fell off ladders—despite safety equipment. Sometimes customers ended up with blood sugar emergencies. Emily was a volunteer first responder for her store. Her training only went as far as first aid, CPR, proper AED use, and under which circumstances to call an ambulance. Modern medicine wasn't an option here.

"Captain, who should fill the role now?" the bald behemoth asked.

Captain? Where? A groan came from the makeshift table, and Emily recognized that voice. Her heart leaped into her throat, and fresh guilt tore into her like a cannonball. It should've been her. He'd already taken a whipping for her, and he hadn't healed from it yet.

"I'll do it." Emily feared her skills wouldn't be enough for the captain, but she absolutely couldn't do nothing.

Her friend cast her a worried stare. "Ye need the doctor yerself. Surely someone more qualified—"

"I might not know how to sail. I might not have the strength to keep up with you, and I might not fit in, but I can do this. I have to do this." Emily moved around Fergus and approached the captain apprehensively. It was different when the patient was someone...she cared about.

The captain groaned with his eyes squeezed shut. Emily was terrified he was going to die because of her. She wished she'd packed more pain meds. "I'm not a doctor, but I'm the best you got. Is there a medicine chest on board?" she asked the behemoth over her shoulder. "And bring me fresh water and a cup." The large man nodded, accepting his orders, and left.

Emily turned to Fergus. "Help him, and bring some clean rags, too." She needed any help she could get, and she wanted privacy.

Fergus reluctantly left, and Emily rolled the barrel seat over to the captain's side and settled the lantern near. She trembled with adrenaline coursing through her as she observed his bloodied tunic. Shards of wood peppered the captain's side. His hand moved to cover the tender site. Holding back her tears, she tried to move his hands to see the injuries clearer, but he resisted. She palmed his shaking hands. "Please," she begged. "Let me see."

The captain's faced was pinched, but he met her gaze and grunted. "I don't want you to see me like this."

"Then you shouldn't have gotten in the way."

Captain Lemoine closed his eyes. "A captain protects his men, and dying to save his men is an honor."

Tears shimmered in her vision. "Don't you dare give up on me. You deserve a better life than this filthy ship, and you deserve a death when you're old. Not like this. Not...like this. Not...for me."

The captain's hands moved away and settled on the plank beneath him. She gently lifted a corner of the fabric, careful not to agitate the wounds, but the captain sucked in breaths and his body tensed. She didn't get a good look, but this was far beyond her pay grade. There was no one else. The tears fell. "Why? Why did you do that?"

His breath hitched and released in spurts.

Scolding him wasn't productive. "Try not to move. I'm going to do everything I can, but you must do as I say."

The captain groaned.

The thunder of boots turned her head, and the beefy behemoth deposited an old wooden chest and a pail of water by her feet. Fergus appeared behind him, white as fresh winter's snow, and he handed her a cup and an armful of rags—not as clean as she'd prefer, but beggars and choosers and all that. They hovered. Emily wanted more alone time with the captain, and having these two lurking over her shoulder wasn't going to help steady her nerves at all. "Go fix the holes in the boat or something."

Both men left, and Emily appreciated them listening to her—as if she were an equal.

The captain managed a chuckle and then another groan. "Taking over my job, are we?"

Emily smiled. "Nope. It's still yours. I'm doing my best." She opened the chest and shifted the lantern. "You need better lighting in this place. This is ridiculous. Who can work like this?"

"Meeks."

"Stop talking. I don't want you to hurt yourself worse."

"Words don't hurt. It's everything else."

Emily gazed at him thoughtfully, but she couldn't waste time talking when she needed to stabilize him. Inside the chest were strips of soiled cloth, glass bottles of uneven size and color with indecipherable labels, and various rusty metal tools she wouldn't know what to do with. Oh, and a pouch of powder. Emily didn't want to know what that was.

Pain management became the top priority. Emily used the cup to scoop out water. Opening her tiny ibuprofen bottle from her pouch, she offered the captain four white pills and the cup. "Swallow these and use this to wash them down."

The captain opened his mouth for the pills, and she set them just inside his lips, trying not to focus too much on the feel of his lips.

And he'd made such a big deal over her trying to feed him chocolate.

Brushing aside a minor amusement, Emily supported his head while the captain drank. She set the cup down and exhaled a deep breath. Next step. Emily slipped the tiny scissors from her sewing kit onto her fingers and lifted the captain's tunic.

"What are...you doing?" He blocked her.

A little humor helped with stress and pain. "I've already seen you half naked. Don't be shy now." His hand didn't move, so Emily resorted to begging. "I can help, but I need to keep the site clear. I need to see what I'm doing. Please let me help."

The captain dropped his head back and removed his hand, fingers curling into fists at his sides.

Emily cut off his tunic and freed the sodden material from the punctures, exposing his strong and tanned chest with a dusting of dark hair. Emily blew out a quick breath and examined his skin. Alongside his ribs, a series of wood fragments from the impact pierced his flesh. The darkening of the skin meant severe bruising was on the way. He needed an operating room. But the combination of her first aid skills and her experience with a sewing needle would have to suffice. How much different could sewing flesh be?

Emily dug into her pouch again and removed a small sewing kit she'd brought along to fix any costume malfunctions. She'd also packed ointment to stave off infection in case of splinters from sudden rough waters or touching the tour ship's rail. She hadn't expected to use these things to save a man's life.

"You might have some broken ribs, and I need to keep cutting." Emily snipped along the side of his breeches, finding the material difficult to split with her tiny scissors meant for thread. The captain didn't stop her. After cutting down to his upper thigh, Emily pulled the flap of fabric back only as far as necessary, keeping his privacy intact. She found more blood from several gashes. Not a fatal amount, but he needed stitches. She pulled out a needle and thread from her sewing kit. What could she sterilize it with?

Price's secret rum! Hopefully, there was some left. "I'll be right back. Don't move."

The captain opened one eye, and the corner of his lips lifted. "Here I'd planned on taking a turn about the deck for fresh air, and you just had to ruin it." He chuckled and his face pinched in pain.

Emily smiled for his sake. Seemed the ibuprofen was helping. "A sense of humor is good for you, but it I mean it—don't move."

"As you wish, captain."

Now was not the time for more Westley devotion. Emily bit back her smile and darted across the lower deck, thankful everyone—including her—had tucked away their hammocks. She ducked and hoped over obstacles and climbed the ladder to the mess hall. She found the last barrel the pirates had, and there was hardly a glisten at the bottom. Emily tilted it and scooped out what she could with a nearby discarded cup. Desperate for more, she checked every mug left behind and dumped all the remainders into her cup. She had half a cup to work with. It would have to do.

Returning to the captain's side at lightning speed, Emily set down the rum and sterilized a needle and thread with it. She paused. He'd need something to bite into. What did she have? Emily used her tiny scissors and cut away some of the hem of her tunic, and tearing when the scissors surrendered. She fastened a string of knots into it. "Bite this. It'll help." She placed the knots between his lips, and he bit down.

"Here it comes. Try not to move." Emily poured a ration of rum over the biggest shard at his hip.

The captain grunted in pain, squeezing down on the knots. With a rubber thimble on her forefinger, she gripped the hunk of wood embedded in his flesh and pulled it out with a smooth stroke. The captain tensed, face burning bright red, cords on his neck straining, and a long groan passed his lips. The sooner she could get through it, the better, for his sake and hers. She poured more rum over the open wound and began the arduous process of stitching the bleeding wound closed.

She spoke to him, not expecting answers, just to help him keep his mind off the pain. "Few men would dive in front of a cannonball for you. Duty or not, I don't understand why you did it."

Another groan passed between his lips. "For the same reason I accepted your punishment in your stead. I couldn't bear to see you harmed."

Emily paused, stunned by his words. She'd begged him not to take her punishment, but she never thanked him. "It wasn't just a captain's duty?"

Captain Lemoine opened his sincere brown eyes, but he didn't answer, and that was answer enough.

"Thank you. You saved my life." Emily's heart pounded in her chest, and her hands shook. She took a quick break to shake the adrenaline from her fingers and noticed what might be tweezers in the doctor's chest. She dunked them into the rum and meticulously pulled out each of the smaller slices of wood, dropping them into a pile by her feet.

He groaned and tilted his head back, squeezing his eyes closed. "How did you learn to doctor?"

Chatting was a distraction. "I like to sew clothing, and this isn't much different. I even made my own clothes."

The captain smiled through the pain. "Then you went to a strange school. I've never seen stitches like those."

"You've never seen stitches like the ones in your thigh, either."

The captain chuckled.

Emily watched his face as she wiped the tweezers clean, giving him a small break. She snipped a fresh length of thread.

"The men on the rigging crew patch up the sails when they tear, but you're not a sailor."

Emily thought a question rested in there. She worked methodically, starting with the next worst injury at his rib, holding it together and securing it closed with pretty stitches. His muscles shifted under her hand, and she wished she could take away all his pain.

The captain's eyes opened and squeezed shut once again. She trickled more rum over the finished product. Not bad for a dimly lit rocking ship in the middle of the Caribbean with a sewing kit.

"The worst is over now. Only a few smaller ones left. Stay with me." From her untrained eye, none of his injuries appeared to have punctured anything vital.

Emily moved on to the minor gashes and stitched them one by one. She slathered antibacterial ointment around each clean wound, taking great care in her touch. She hoped he didn't succumb to infection.

"The answer is no," he said.

"To what question?"

His chest rose and fell with short breaths. "It wasn't my duty."

Emily captured his gaze and froze with a roll of what could be called gauze in her hand.

"Emile Porter…I can't thank you enough for what you've done for me. At a tumultuous precipice in my career, you saved my life from a mutinous crew, you gave me the chance to earn back their confidence, and now you're saving my life again. I don't have such luck with non-sailor conscripts, but I daresay I'm grateful to have you on my ship."

She was under the impression she only mastered the art of screwing up. "I'm glad I was here for you." Emily's face burned hot, surprised at her own admission. She didn't belong here. She wasn't supposed to be here. She clearly didn't fit in, but Emily was thinking of nothing but him.

14

Chapter 14

"HELP ME SIT UP," the captain asked.

"That's a good idea. Then I can wrap you with this." Emily held out what appeared to be a roll of gauze and set it off to the side. She braced herself for getting very personal with the captain. On an exhale, Emily straddled the captain's lap carefully, keeping too much distance between their bodies. The captain's gaze was unmistakable—there was heat and lust hidden behind all the pain. Warmth flooded her cheeks and sweat broke out on her back. Emily leaned in by his face and scooped her arms under his. Her body trembled. She wanted to press him against her and kiss those smooth lips of his. Their faces were inches apart. All she'd have to do was move a little.

She couldn't.

He'd definitely discover two things that didn't belong, and maybe a few things that were missing.

"Gently now. I don't need you tearing your new stitches. On three." Emily counted down and eased the captain upright.

His handsome face pinched, but he maintained a seated position on his own. He swung his legs down over the edge of the plank and winced, sliced fabrics draping haphazardly. Captain Lemoine shucked the rest of his tunic scraps.

Emily uncurled the gauze, appreciating the view of his upper body and exposed thick thigh. But her heart broke all over again at the train tracks of stitches running over his side. Those should've been hers. "Arms up, if you can."

The captain held his arms away from his gorgeous torso, and Emily leaned in close again, wrapping him to support his ribs. His eyes followed her as she moved her arms around and around, pulling the material supportively taut. "How does that feel?"

"It's missing something."

"What's that?" Emily thought she'd thought of everything. Sure, some morphine would've been nice, but that wasn't an option—

The captain closed the distance between them, his lips finding hers. His fingers rested on the nape of her neck and moved down to her back.

Emily's brows lifted. Her hands slipped along that soft scruff of his beard and held him close as she repositioned their lips, unwilling to let him go. They were as soft as she'd imagined, and he moved with care, testing her, questioning her.

Asking permission to be there.

Their breaths mingled, and Emily fought every carnal desire to leap at him and take him here on this dirty plank. As if their thoughts were one, Captain Lemoine pulled her closer.

Emily pushed against his efforts and backed away. She needed an excuse. Thankfully, there were several to choose from. "That's against the rules."

"Some rules were meant to be broken." The fiery heat in the captain's eyes was alluring, and she agreed wholeheartedly.

But breaking the most grievous of offenses wouldn't be excused with a single punishment, and the captain could handle no more. Her face pinched in confusion.

"What is the matter?" Captain Lemoine asked, dark eyes of concern flickering under candlelight.

He'd said he wanted her to reject him, but this was just the opposite. "Why did you kiss me?"

"I've sailed these seas for five and twenty years with my eye focused on one goal. Along the way, I've commandeered ships, I've recruited men to the account and lost many on the way. I've always been sure of what my purpose was. But as we progress through seasons in our lives, sometimes the life we've always seen changes when we least expect it. I want to know everything about you. I want to spend every moment with you, and the distance between was too much to bear. I kissed you because I am simply weak—no longer able to resist your allure. Emile Porter, I understand this might be different for you, but I want you, and I want you to be comfortable about it."

A warmth blossomed in her chest. She'd never felt more wanted in her life, and the feeling was mutual. Emily desperately wanted to be with him and be by his side, but how? They were from different worlds. And if he discovered she wasn't a man, would the captain still want her? And at her deceit, would he turn her in for the just punishment? It was a risk she couldn't take. "As long as we're both on this ship, we can't."

The bald behemoth lumbered into the tiny room and lit up with the sight. "Captain! Good to see you upright."

"Cantu, what is the status on the man-o'-war?"

"She's found terrible winds, I'm afraid." Cantu, the enormous man, grinned. "Most unfortunate about our prizes."

"Most excellent. Tell the men I'll be up shortly and not to worry."

Cantu nodded and gleefully left.

"I hope you have a change of clothing," Emily said, admiring the view while it lasted.

The captain looked down at himself. "I do, in my quarters. Please accompany me."

CAPTAIN ERIC LEMOINE HAD always been sure of what he wanted, always prepared to do whatever necessary to get it. The kiss had been the only thing in the world needed to dull his pain, but it would be the only one he'd ever get. Lemoine would remain on this ship until that one goal was met, and he wanted Emile at his side, but he couldn't ask Emile to wait for him. The handsome man was the first person Lemoine had ever wanted, but he couldn't have him. Lemoine should not have broken his own request to remain at arm's length. Now Lemoine could never let go.

Still, he had to.

Emile helped him to his feet and wrapped an arm around him for support. Lemoine groaned as he straightened. He was in worse shape than he'd thought.

As Emile took small steps, they found a slow rhythm to make their way up, and the handsome man's face was so close to his own, it pained him to not kiss him again.

"I thought pirate captains were supposed to be ruthless, evil, devils of the sea, enemies of every nation," Emile said near his ear.

"That's mostly the tales."

Emile stopped and turned his face to his. The distance, so little but so far at the same time, pressed a knife in his chest.

"Absorbing damage costs the crew in more ways than one, so intimidating ships into surrendering is a much wiser strategy. But that effect is the result of a carefully grown reputation. Only on rare occasions are deaths necessary."

"You never answered why you shot Captain Sinclair when you already doomed to die."

Captain Lemoine didn't want to withhold the truth from Emile. He'd put his trust in him, and as much as Lemoine wanted to learn everything about the puzzling man, Lemoine wanted to be known, too. He wanted to matter to someone. But if Lemoine couldn't have Emile, what was the point in offering a tale that could tarnish his reputation if shared?

Lemoine turned the questioning back onto Emile, hitting a place he knew the man wouldn't answer. "You're a very strange man, Emile. I cannot place it, and I wish you'd help me understand."

Emile gazed into his face with a softness and a pain of his own. "Let's get you dressed."

As expected, he'd avoided. Lemoine nodded, and Emile led the way, but he struggled with the listing of the ship, and he used bulkheads and other handholds to make his way on his feet. Too many times the cut material in his breeches sent a cool breeze where it didn't belong. Lemoine tried to keep himself proper, but he wasn't always successful. He'd never felt more like an invalid, but next to Emile, he wasn't embarrassed. He was grateful. The man understood the lengths Lemoine had gone for him, the cause of this pain.

Despite the cavern between them, he'd do it all over again without a second's thought.

At the main deck, Emile helped him stand up, supporting him from the uninjured side, and he brought Lemoine across the deck.

"Captain's on his feet! Everyone, captain's back to bring us to glory!" A chorus of cheers sang across the decks, and suddenly the men were in higher spirits and working faster. The captain smiled and waved to the men to show his strength.

Jettisoning the hold to outrun the Royal Navy meant they had nothing to sell. After they restocked their lost supplies in Nassau, the men would be eager to return to the seas to fetch a prize. And Captain Lemoine would lead them to the glory he'd promised.

Emily took much of the captain's weight up the decks and across to his navigation room and into his cabin. Inside the humid hull, and under the blistering sun, Emily was sweating. She'd held him a little awkwardly to prevent a boob graze, too. And she was already long overdue for a shower. Emily carefully set him on the bed, and Captain Lemoine adjusted the loose flap of his breeches to cover himself more appropriately. Emily wished for a better view, and the captain had put the option on the table, but Emily couldn't.

"In my trunk."

Emily unlatched the intricate trunk and chose a tunic and a pair of breeches. Emily figured out he hadn't been wearing anything underneath his breeches, but that didn't mean he didn't have any. While carefully searching for drawers, Emily couldn't help but fawn over the materials, the stitching...the quality. Cosplayers would die for such authentic attire.

Emily was already fangirling.

"Is something the matter?" Captain Lemoine asked.

She'd lingered too long. Her face flushed, and she closed the trunk, standing with her arms full. "Can you put on your clothes, or do you need help?"

"I will speak the truth, but it shall not leave the confines of this room, understand?"

He had her full attention. "I understand."

"I need a grown man to help me dress. Thank you for your help."

Emily smiled. "It's okay." She reached for the hem of his tunic, and the captain flinched as he raised his arms. Emily quickly removed the destroyed tunic, and to irritate the wounds as little as possible, she slipped the fresh tunic straight on. She'd already seen his chest and abs, but she didn't skip a chance to get another eyeful.

Emily reached for the waistband of his mangled breeches. "Can you lift, and I'll tug?"

"I cannot," he said, with an embarrassed tone.

Emily had to keep his dignity intact. This was difficult for him, but it wasn't difficult for her. He was magnificent and beautiful, and she relished the opportunity to help. Emily fished out her sewing kit and slipped her tiny scissors into her fingers. She cut the air apologetically. "They're already sliced up. I don't see any other way."

"Proceed." The captain watched her intently with each snip.

Could she have cut them off with only the metal grazing his skin? Yes, of course. Did she? No, of course not. Safety first. Emily began where she'd left off, cutting near his injuries, with a finger carefully keeping his skin protected.

The captain's head fell back as if he, too, enjoyed her touch.

After finishing the already damaged side, she moved to his other side and cut all the way down, one snip at a time. Her fingers ached and cramped, but she didn't care. She dragged a hand along his healthy thigh, lifting the fabric for each cut.

The damaged fabric twitched, and knowing what the captain was thinking, Emily blew air up her face while her heart pounded ferociously in her chest.

She freed his feet from his boots and brought the breeches over. "Ready?"

The captain nodded.

Emily moved the fabric away, exposing him entirely. His thighs were as firm as she'd pictured, mounds of muscle gave him a nice shape. And he was well hung, judging by the half mast down below.

Emily bit back a smile, and sweat trickled down her back. She exhaled and kneeled at his feet. Emily slipped the fresh pair up to his knees. "You'll have to stand up to finish putting them on."

"When you're ready." His features pinched.

"The question is, are you ready?" Emily wished she'd checked her phone for the time, so she'd known when to give him another dose of painkillers. Without a functional network, she doubted the time would be right, anyway. Emily moved over to his good side and counted down to three. She lifted with all her might, arms trembling with the effort.

She bent and lifted his breeches. The captain eagerly tied them as the door opened, but her face was near his bulge. Quartermaster Price scowled.

"It's not what you think," Emily volunteered.

Price scrutinized her and turned to his captain. "Glad to see you on your feet, Lemoine. When you're ready, we'll set a new course for Nassau. Porter, we owe you a great debt."

"Please, no. It's no big deal." Earning praise from the man who wanted to whip her a few days ago felt so jarring, so superficial. She didn't believe his gratitude.

"We haven't assigned to you a position yet," Price added. "Since you have a doctor's skills, and we happen to be short one, you'll do just fine."

"Wait, what?" Emily barked out in surprise and looked at the captain for his rebuttal. She belonged assisting with the sails next to Fergus.

But Captain Lemoine only nodded. From one moment to the next, she had no idea where she ranked on the totem pole of the ship. From a welcomed recruit to a rule-breaking amateur in need of scolding and punishment, to a fair sailor. Now she was the doctor.

"And since the captain is in such terrible condition, you'll have to stay by his side during shore leave."

Emily's mouth fell open. Her eyes moved to the captain, whose fiery gaze was plain on his face. If she was glued to his side, how was she going to get a shower?

"I take it this isn't a problem?" Price asked.

Emily shook her head. "No, not at all. Sorry. I'm just surprised by the promotion."

"I'll leave you to it." Price pointedly glared at her and the captain's waist, where he'd just finished tying his breeches. He closed the door on his way out, without another word.

"Is it such a burden to assist me ashore?" The captain asked with a mischievous glint in his eye.

"You know I'm not a real doctor, right?"

The captain smiled. "Better than the carpenter." Carpenters, good with hand tools—namely saws—were frequently moved into the position when the skills were required. Emily wasn't sure if that was a compliment or not. Their bar was so low.

"Ready to set the course?" she asked playfully. Emily actually felt like she belonged, and it put a spring in her step.

"Let's get to it."

Emily gripped the captain and assisted his steps, pausing when his ribs or his thigh wound hurt too much. They didn't have to move too far. The navigation room was next door.

That meant any noises made inside the captain's quarters could be heard by any of the navigation crew. Something to be mindful of.

After she moved him into the next room, only then Emily realized she'd forgotten to retrieve her necklace from the shredded clothing.

Chapter 15

WHEN THE CITY OF Nassau glided into view the next day, the crew cheered. Emily gripped an oar and helped paddle ashore on a longboat, carrying a dozen pirates and the injured captain, while other longboats formed a line behind. They disembarked by rank, and since she was assigned to the captain's recovery, that gave her a position of authority.

As a retail worker bee, Emily was passive-aggressively scolded for not picking up shifts on her day off, forced to work most holidays, frequently denied unpaid vacations, but as thanks, gift cards and pizza parties were dangled for motivation. It was weird to be held in esteem, to be respected and admired. Here everyone mattered, and anyone stepping out of line—even if it was the captain—was corrected and the work continued in mutual agreement. From nothing, the pirates had created their own society that treated everyone fairly.

And yet, the Crown had destroyed them all—both in reputation and in sentencing to death. The Crown feared losing its power, a common theme in her modern world.

But seeing land for the first time in what felt like too long, she sighed in relief at the approaching solid ground. With sadness, Emily realized her pining for the sea had its limits—like any vacation would. The call of home was strong. And when she returned home, Emily expected the historical research would no longer hold the glamour it once did. She would have to write her own firsthand account of life aboard a pirate ship, but then what? Move on to a new hobby? She wouldn't know where to start.

More importantly, would she miss the Caribbean, the *Sea Lion*, and...Captain Lemoine so much the pining would be worse?

Eventually, she'd get that answer.

As the longboat coasted up to the dock, a pair of sailors knotted lines, securing the boat to the pilings. The others climbed out, but the captain waited back. Emily reached under him, and he stood with a wince. Muscular Cantu tried to clap hands and assist his exit from the wobbling boat, but Captain Lemoine refused. "I want the doctor to help, lest I break more bones in the process."

"Of course, sir. Pardon me." The helpful Cantu instead stabilized the rocking boat, and when the captain's feet touched the solid dock, the sailor helped the next longboat unload. Emily held the captain still and upright while the men gathered and headed off. They needed to restock supplies—particularly the rum. Since they'd dumped the contents of the hold to escape the Royal Navy, Emily hoped they had enough coin on hand to purchase—not steal—those necessities.

Flushed from rowing and exhilarated to be on stable ground, Emily secured Captain Lemoine's arm around her shoulder and waited for the captain's pain to ease. He'd saved her life. The least she could do was be patient. "Are you ready?"

"As much as I can be. Now that you're here, what do you want to do?"

Emily didn't expect the captain to ask about her needs, but perhaps they could both get what they wanted. "Let's find somewhere to rest," Emily insisted. "And I would love a bath."

"The Golden Macaw it is," the captain said in her ear, sending a shiver down her sweaty back. "Just beyond the blacksmith. Marta shall provide us the usual room."

This was Nassau, a famous pirate haven, and likely everyone knew everyone else. Emily wondered what stories Marta must have, what stories this town harbored beneath the surface, the ones that never made the history books. Emily shuffled along through sand and stone paths, feet itching for a hot soak, but all she could do was absorb the history in front of her. Townspeople strolled around them, some carrying goods on their heads in baskets, and others emptyhanded. One walked a goat on a leash. Emily stared at its little tail swishing, and she laughed. It was so weirdly cute, but she refrained from stopping to pet it.

"What's amusing you this time?" Captain Lemoine asked with a hint of playfulness, despite his pain.

"I've never seen a goat in person before."

The captain smiled at her in disbelief. "And the puzzle grows."

"What?"

"How is it possible you've never seen a goat?"

"Me and my mother were too broke to afford any luxuries, and that meant no traveling to the zoo. No movies. No shopping for fun. For vacations, we went camping. And on the weekends, we picnicked and spent time at city parks."

And that was why Tyler's theft hurt so deeply. It wasn't just the money. Stealing from people was never about the money. Money could be lost. Money could be made. The importance was what that money represented, what sentimentality the object held. Stealing tore something away from a person, disrespected their time earning it, damaged their soul. That money was her future, because she'd never had a past. And Tyler stole it. Emily couldn't accept thievery on any scale.

So while pretending to be a man, signing pirate articles, and playing doctor to an injured pirate captain who'd saved her life were all things she'd never dreamed of experiencing, that goat brought a tear to her eye.

"You weren't raised in privilege?" Captain Lemoine asked, surprised.

"Not at all."

The handsome man captured her gaze and worry filled his brow. "Why the tears? What's wrong, Emile?"

Emily smiled. "My mother would've wanted to pet the goat."

"Where is she now?" he asked gently.

"She passed a few years back."

"I'm so very sorry for your loss." The captain winced with a misstep and stopped in place.

"Are you all right?" she asked.

"We're here."

Above them was a painted wood sign reading The Golden Macaw. Men entered and exited the front door, and Emily waited until she could bring them across the threshold with no one pushing them to move faster. Several of the patrons lifted brows at her and the captain's situation.

"Lemoine?" One man stopped in front of them. He appeared to be in his mid-forties, hair thinning and waist widening. He tilted his head and beamed in recognition of a long-lost friend. His hand jutted out in greeting. "How've you been, mate?"

The captain shook carefully, and the friend was gentle enough not to further injure the captain. "Wilcox. Good to see you."

"Are you staying a while this time?" Wilcox eyed Emily for a brief moment, but otherwise didn't seem interested in meeting her.

"Long enough to restock, I'm afraid. Then back out to sea."

Wilcox smiled. "Word is spreading like fleas. Don't expect to be the only ones there. If I were going to make that attempt, I'd bring extra guns."

The captain nodded his gratitude for the vague advice. "Pardon us now, Wilcox. I have healing to do."

"Good luck on your account." Wilcox nodded and walked off.

Emily saw an opportunity in the tavern's doorway, and she swept the captain inside and straight into a cloud of tobacco smoke. Emily coughed. Potted palms rested in the corners of the open space. To the left was a registration desk with a broad stairwell leading up to the open second-story balcony. At the opposite end of the lobby was a bar, and in between were round tables. Butter yellow and soft green paint was flaking off the walls and banisters, but Emily loved the atmosphere.

A voluptuous woman approached. Her long hair was curled and piled high on her head. She wore an extravagant dress that looked more like a colorful bridal gown, and Emily couldn't image how she'd gotten into it or how she used the bathroom. The woman's friendly smile meant she was familiar with the captain also, and Emily presumed she was the hostess of the establishment. Emily followed the woman's gaze to the captain, and he smiled back. Familiar old friends, it seemed.

The woman leaned in for a hug, but Emily didn't want to let go. Her skin hummed with just the proximity. Besides, she still supported the captain's weight and couldn't stabilize him quickly enough to trust letting go. The woman moved in too close and personal. Loose curls tickled her face, and Emily blew them away, wishing her breath blew the woman herself away. No such luck. The woman released her embrace and placed her hand on Captain Lemoine's upper arm as if clinging to him like a dog.

What had gotten into Emily? Actual jealousy over this strange woman was rolling through her like fire. It must've been too much sun and the after effects of a concussion.

"Lemoine! How nice to see you again. Right this way, and I'll have your room ready for you." She turned her head and shouted, "Sarah! Captain Lemoine's room now!"

A young demure woman across the lobby dipped her head, lifted her skirts, and brushed upstairs.

Marta returned her attention to the captain, but she still hadn't released him. "Oh, honey. I'm so glad you've returned. Brought the entire crew, didn't you?" A slender finger caressed his arm. "How long will you be staying?"

Emily's concussion-induced possessiveness spiked. "The captain is injured. As his caretaker, I'd appreciate you not touching him."

Marta's brows popped, and she assessed Emily up and down, as if seeing her for the first time. Her gaze flicked back and forth between the two of them. As a knowing smile lifted her lips almost imperceptibly, the wheels in her head turned. For some reason, Emily read condescension in her expression. So much for that respect and admiration.

The captain spoke up, "Marta, this is my doctor, Emile Porter. I expect his needs shall be met. Do I make myself clear?"

Emily didn't like the sound of that. Her eyes swept the place in a new light. This wasn't just a motel. "That's not...no. That's unnecessary."

"It's necessary. Trust me," the captain insisted.

"No, it's really not."

Marta's smile spread as she watched their banter. Emily wanted to tell her to butt out.

"Emile," the captain countered with a playful interest. "Isolation at sea affects a man. You need some relaxation away from the brain-scrambling swaying of the ship. If you have no experience, Marta's ladies know how to do it right." The captain met Marta's eyes, and she nodded in agreement.

"I don't need ladies. All I want is a hot bath and some privacy. That I will gladly accept."

The captain said, "You're going to draw a bath for yourself? Carry the buckets at the right temperature all the way up the stairs from the stove?"

Emily's mouth opened. That wasn't what she thought at all.

"Marta, have a hot bath drawn for us." The captain smiled with a tease. He'd been playing with her.

This place must've been a motel as she'd first thought, and there was nothing in Price's orders that said she had to share a room. "Us?" Emily repeated, eyes wide.

"We're sharing a room. Price's orders—you must stay by my side."

Emily's mouth opened.

Lemoine leaned into her ear. "Unless you have the funds for the room next door."

The few bucks Emily had brought to the festival would be worth absolutely nothing here. She gave him a tight smile. "Can you handle the stairs?"

Captain Lemoine chuckled. "Broken bones never hindered me before."

Emily didn't want to think about the Captain having suffered severe injuries previously. "We'll take one room."

Marta nodded with a sweet grin. Emily led them both to the foot of the stairs. To preserve his pride, Emily counted prior to lifting up each step, so the captain could brace himself. Step after painfully slow step, they climbed up to the second-story balcony. "Why couldn't we have a ground-floor room?"

The captain smiled through his pain and pointed to the room Sarah had brushed into. "This one."

Emily brought them inside and set him gently onto the mattress. He fell back onto layers of plush bedding, legs hanging off the end. Emily crouched down and unlaced his boots without thinking twice about it.

"What in the devil are you doing?" he asked, head lifting.

"Taking off your boots so you can rest."

The captain's head fell back. "This place is more public than my private quarters, and you surprised me, but thank you."

Sarah and another young woman knocked on the door, holding pails. Without waiting for an invitation, they swept into the room and dumped their pails of steaming water into a tub. Emily sighed, wishing to strip down and soak to wash away the saltwater.

"A change of clothing would be amazing," Emily said to herself, feeling the layers of modern polyester and salty leather clinging to her skin.

"Bring one set of slops and charge it to my room," the captain said.

"What? That's unnecessary. I couldn't ask that," Emily backpedaled.

"Take your bath," Captain Lemoine said. "Enjoy fresh clothing. We're here for a reason, and I'm not going anywhere."

Emily caught the women before they left. "Is there a privacy screen somewhere?"

Sarah returned to the tub without a word and drew forth a folding partition. With a simple nod, they two women left silently, as if to be seen and not heard.

"Men of the sea are not bashful," the captain said while staring at the ceiling. "You'll adjust, eventually."

Not *likely*, Emily thought.

One woman immediately returned, as if a closet was next to the door, and set a folded stack of clothes on a table just inside the room. While lying on the bed, the captain gestured his acknowledgment. Sarah left again, closing the door behind her.

"Go, enjoy yourself," the captain said.

"And you're going to stay right there?" Emily retrieved the stack of clothing.

"I have no intentions of escaping you."

Emily smiled and hid behind the partition. That wasn't what she'd meant.

"Can you satisfy me one question?" the captain called over from the bed.

Emily unlaced her jerkin and peeled off her sticky shirt. "Sure."

"Where are you from?"

She'd dodged the question last time, so she gave him the lie she told Captain Sinclair, calling over the partition, "An island off the coast of the colonies."

Emily unfastened her breeches and pulled them down, and trusting he wasn't near, she slipped out of her underwear and the tank top with molded cups. If Lemoine saw her like this—naked, exposed, clearly not a man, the betrayal would be irreparable. Memories of Tyler berating her because she couldn't be trusted only added to the weight on her shoulders. And since she'd signed the articles, she'd be sentenced to 'suffer death'. Emily didn't want to think of the different ways they'd carry out that sentence, or Price's face while doing it. Or Captain Lemoine's. He probably wouldn't want her anymore, knowing she didn't have the right 'equipment'.

Emily couldn't change what she'd already done; there was no point in dwelling on the 'what ifs'. She could only move forward, and that began with cleaning herself.

Emily dipped into the tub with a gentle swish of water. A sensual groan escaped her lips as a soothing warmth massaged the sore aches and salty sweat. Her nerves melted away. The water wasn't super warm, but since she'd been sweating, it didn't matter. It was fresh water. Emily untied the red rag on her head and let down her blonde hair. She dunked her head under and surfaced, pushing the wet strands back.

"Which one?" the captain asked. He was still on the bed, judging by the carry in his voice.

Emily scrubbed her arms and legs, and hung her hand off the back of her neck, massaging the aching muscles from carrying a man's weight on one side. She pinched her face in thought. "One off the coast of Florida." His stubbornness in refusing to drop the subject was frustrating. She didn't know what to tell him that he'd believe, so there was no point in raising alarms. Emily just wanted to clean up in peace.

16

Chapter 16

Captain Eric Lemoine knew Emile was lying. Instead of angering him, Lemoine began to worry. Was Emile running from something? Hiding from someone? If he were in trouble, Lemoine had every intention of solving it. Soon he could solve anything. "I daresay your continued dance around the question is only intriguing me more."

As expected, Emile didn't answer.

Captain Lemoine pulled himself upright, against doctor's orders, he thought with a sly smile, and rose to his feet. Every muscle from his chest to his knees ached as if he'd taken the shot directly. If he had, he'd been wrapped and tossed into the sea like poor Meeks. Lemoine was grateful his injuries weren't worse. And he was...grateful to Emile, the beautiful, puzzling man with a heart of gold. Terrible sailor, but he was a quick learner.

Had Lemoine been too forward when he'd kissed Emile? His response to Lemoine's pouring of affections had been, 'As long as we're both on this ship, we can't.' Well, they were no longer on the ship, but Emile still wasn't opening up. Had it been an excuse to push him away without hurting him? On the contrary, granting that sliver of hope was cruel if it hadn't been true.

He risked tearing stitches to seek information that would settle his heart.

Did someone already have Emile's?

With one hand reaching uselessly in the air for support that wasn't there, Lemoine shuffled over to the privacy screen. "If you care not to share that detail, can you tell me who your companion, Miss Angela, is? Someone dear to you?"

Lemoine leaned against the screen, careful not to topple it, and gazed upon Emile in the bath. What he found both answered many questions, but also angered him. Emile's face was flushed from the warmth of the bath, so when his—or Lemoine should say 'her'—arms covered her chest, he couldn't tell just how shamed she was.

"I—I can explain..." Emile stuttered. "It's not what you think."

Wet strands of hair clung to her face and narrow shoulders. Her thin arms. Her smooth jaw. Her beautiful face. It all made sense. How could he have missed such a truth before him? Part of his anger was on himself. He should've known.

"It's not?" Captain Lemoine couldn't keep the curt tone from his voice. "Please explain why a woman infiltrated my ship and lied to everyone."

Emile—not likely her name at all—looked down, unable to meet his gaze. "You wouldn't believe me if I told you."

Fury raged through his shredded veins. Not just for the breaking of Lemoine's heart, but also for Emile's sake. The consequences were dire. "Is that what you meant? You'd said we couldn't be together so long as we were on the *Sea*

Lion. This is why, isn't it? You wouldn't expose the truth to me. You didn't trust me."

Her face lifted, showing disbelief. "That's what you're angry about? That I didn't tell a *pirate* captain I was a woman, when I signed on the line acknowledging I'd be *killed* for it? I knew the consequences, so how I was supposed to trust you with that information? And for the record, you kissed me, and that's against the rules, too."

She had a point. "Why did you sign?"

"I needed to stay on that ship long enough to get my necklace back. If I hadn't, I wouldn't be sitting here right now."

Lemoine was sure she would be here, still hounding him for that jewel, only her life wouldn't be in his hands. He still couldn't reconcile every piece of the Emile puzzle. "And this Angela, was she your traveling chaperone?"

"Angela is my best friend, and she's missing," Emile said, and with a dry tone, she added, "I don't need a chaperone."

Lemoine couldn't even relish in the knowledge Emile's heart had not been taken. Emile broke rules everywhere she went, which led him to want to know where she was from even more, but he wouldn't get that answer. The captain shook his head in disbelief. "Two women traveling alone."

What was he going to do with their new doctor? Emile had value, but he was burdened with exposing her betrayal and having her punished. The punishment was worse than dire. It was death. But even after this grave revelation, Lemoine couldn't see Emile killed. Resigned, he said on a sigh, "I accepted your punishment in your stead, and I bore the brunt of the shot's blast to keep you safe. I couldn't bear to see you harmed then."

"But now that I'm a woman, you don't see me the same way?" Emile asked cautiously.

"I don't." Lemoine wanted her more than ever, but now he couldn't have her.

Emile's face paled, and if Lemoine hadn't known better, he'd almost believe Emile was...heartbroken. Lemoine added gently, "But I still can't see you harmed. You can't return to the ship."

Emile stood, panic on her face. Water ran down her smooth naked body, and Lemoine didn't know what to do. He just marveled at the sight while it lasted.

"But...I'm your doctor. I need to help you heal," Emile said with rising tones, realized the blunder of standing before him, and sank back into the water. Lemoine happened to enjoy the view.

But she had a point again. Lemoine had been injured in battle many times before, but not quite this seriously, and if he could have a doctor on his arm tending his every need, he'd be unwise to dismiss such benefit. But to bring her aboard meant he would now risk his life as well as hers. For Lemoine to entertain the idea of protecting her once again, at great risk and benefit to himself, he wanted more from her. "Why did you risk mutilation, desertion, and death for a single jewel? What about your home is worth all that?"

Lemoine hoped the answer rested in something he could fix. A man he could hunt down. Seeds he could purchase. Land he could recover. Lemoine was all too familiar with the need to bring home something valuable. Soon, Lemoine would have all he needed to solve any problem, even his own.

"It's my only way to get home."

Lemoine didn't know how to work with that, but Emile was nothing if not obtuse. A spike of pain had his face pinching. Lemoine leaned harder on the screen, and Emile stood, wrapped a towel around her chest to her knees, and rushed to his side.

Emile supported Lemoine and brought him back to the bed. He didn't fight her. She saw all his vulnerability already.

Emile sat next to him. "Here's how this is going to go. We're both getting back on that ship, and you'll give me my necklace. I promise to help you heal so long as you need me, but the moment you don't or issues with the crew become too dangerous, I'll disappear. Then you can lead your men to rescue the next merchant crew in distress."

"I can't do that," Lemoine said, staring at his scarred hands.

Chapter 17

EMILY DRAGGED A HAND through her wet hair. Sitting in nothing but a towel next to the captain, she was keenly aware of how little was between them. But it didn't matter. The captain didn't feel the same about her now that she was a woman. Emily had expected it, but that didn't make it hurt less. She was thankful Lemoine didn't immediately call the crew over, strip her in front of them for proof, and have her tied up for whatever creative death Price could conjure. But she didn't understand which part of her plan he was rejecting.

"What do you mean?" she asked with an edge to her voice.

"I can't do that," he repeated, softly.

His withholding the necklace meant she couldn't go home, but it angered her more that she couldn't make that decision for herself. The sharpness in her tone returned. "You can't kill me for being a woman who broke the articles, or can't let me go home?"

"I've sailed these waters as a captain ten years now." Captain Lemoine stared at his palms, a sincerity evaporated her anger. "My crew turned over more than once in that time. Some accounts were more successful than others. This crew has been on the verge of mutiny for weeks, whispers of losing my wits to find the best prizes, and you saved me from that. Despite your undermining my authority." He sent her a small lift of his lips.

Intrigued at the captain opening up to her, she asked, "How did you pacify them before?"

"Promises. But my ledger of promises has been red for some time. And that night, I had no promises left to give. I cannot thank you enough." He turned to her with a wince, gentle and vulnerable, breaking her heart. "And I cannot continue to use them."

"I don't need your promise then, and I don't want you to risk your life for mine again, understood?" Emily asked, guilt pouring out of her. His words sounded like a refusal, and she couldn't give up her only way back on that ship. "Just like before. You go on believing I'm a man, and we move forward with the plan I just laid out."

"Why don't you want help? It's strange to me a woman in need would be so fiercely against it."

Emily exhaled, relieved to give the man some truth, and maybe he'd agree for pity's sake. "My father abandoned my mother when I was young. My mother spent all her time working to keep a roof over our heads. Independence was ingrained in me. When I was old enough to work myself, I put all my effort into earning money with the hopes of changing my life someday for both of us. Then I met a man not long ago who made me promises."

The captain said nothing, just held her eye contact, waiting for her to continue.

"I could see a life of comfort I'd never known. My mother could finally quit working. But it wasn't to be. She passed away, and Tyler stole all my money. I'm broke."

"Both the men in your life are imbeciles. What kind of man abandon's his child? His wife? His lover?" Captain Lemoine's hand touched her thigh, and her veins sizzled with heat. "I don't think I want to know where you're from after all. I may not stop myself from teaching them a lesson."

She wished so much he wasn't gay. She wanted to kiss him for just listening, and that possessiveness light a fire in her chest. It was a strange feeling, like he still cared. "It wasn't all Tyler's fault. I was blindly excited about the business venture, and he asked for the money—a little at first, and then more and more. When I wasn't comfortable handing over everything I had, he continued with the promises. A week after I drained my account for him, he came back for more. I said I didn't have any left, that I'd given it all to him. He said he couldn't trust me to do what the business needed when it needed it. All I wanted was a few dollars back to pay a bill."

Emily's lips lifted. "If he would've given it, I'd still be in that cycle of promises, more money handed over, and no business yet."

"You were very generous. It's not your fault a thief manipulated you."

"I thought I loved him. I thought he loved me, and that we were going to be partners. But I broke up with him instead. He still hasn't paid me."

"It's a fortunate end," the captain said, jaw tightening. "You deserve better."

His kindness melted her like the chocolate in her pouch. Seeing he needed a pick-me-up just as much as she did, she opened the pouch and unwrapped a bite size chocolate.

"You need this more than I do. Take it, and no, it's not stolen."

His brow creased. "Then where did you get it?"

"Back home, and I'm offering you a piece." He didn't move, so Emily shook it for emphasis.

"I can see how my words hurt you deeply. I don't believe you're a thief at all," he said gravely, as if the guilt burdened him. "For the necklace or this chocolate."

"Thank you." Damn it. Why did he have to be so sweet?

"In my defense, it's less shocking that a *woman* carries chocolate and a necklace on her person." He smiled wryly and leaned toward her fingers, parting his lips. Emily's heart pounded as she placed the treat in his mouth, and his lips captured her fingers and slid them free.

Captain Lemoine stared at her wide eyed as he chewed. "It's amazing. Very sweet and smooth. With a pleasurable silky texture. I've never tasted anything like it. Thank you for sharing your little luxury with me."

Emily smiled proudly, lifted off the bed, and gently pushed him down onto the mattress. "You need to rest, and we can return to the ship together."

He allowed her to position him comfortably, and his body relaxed on the mattress. "Promises are meaningless to you, so I *don't* promise your secret is safe with me." Despite his pain, he smiled for her. "Don't leave, doctor."

"I won't," she said. Emily flipped up a sheet over his body and took a long look at the man who'd saved her twice—from a brutal merchant captain and a military cannonball—and now he promised to keep her secret to save her life and his position. She was almost home-free. Emily smiled and stepped out onto the balcony.

EMILY LEANED HER FOREARMS on the balcony railing. The crowd below bustled through the smokey haze of the bar restaurant below. A stomach-growling scent of grilled meat wafted up. Men drank and played cards. Coins rattled on the floor. Women in billowing gowns served them fresh drinks and mouth-watering plates with pleasant smiles. A shout below focused her attention on a table below. A small group of the crew gripped their mugs, enjoying the establishment's entertainment. She could hardly believe many of them wanted to toss the captain overboard. He was such a wonderful man.

"There ye are," Fergus climbed the remaining stairs and leaned against the railing next to her shoulder. "I've been looking fur ye. Crew's been wondering if ye dispatched th'weakened captain."

Emily scowled. "Of course not."

Fergus chuckled. "I think it was said in jest." He glanced down below, watching the spectacle of laughing men telling stories.

Emily remembered Fergus's eagerness to escape the crew. "Why are you here? The captain fulfilled his promise to give you safe passage to Nassau. You're free."

"I canny leave before trying tae bring ye tae yer senses. Now's yer chance tae escape these ruffians fur good."

While the captain slept, Emily didn't feel comfortable leaving him, and since she had nothing better to do, chatting with her friend was better than being alone. "And go where?"

"I'll arrange fur a position oan a plantation oan th'other side o' th'island, or if ye prefer, I could be a fisherman. It disny matter tae me which." He was serious.

Emily squinted at him. That wasn't casual planning. "Why are you talking like this?"

"What dae ye mean?"

"Like my opinion on your life counts."

Fergus leaned into her ear. "I know ye're a lassy."

Emily lips parted, and she covered her mouth with her hand. "How? Why haven't you...? How!" She had been so careful. Even the captain never suspected.

"A man traveling wi' a necklace would immediately declare it's a gift fur a woman. Ye never attempted tae lift a barrel of rum. Ye struggled wi' a single bag o' sand. Th'curve o' yer face is just a little too feminine tae be convincing. But I knew right away, which is why I was helping ye." His hand brushed against her jaw with affection, and Emily pulled back. "I have money. I can support us until I find employment. Come wi' me, and ye'll be safe."

"Fergus, you've been a good friend, and I appreciate the offer, but..." she trailed off when his demeanor shifted. He didn't like her answer.

"Ye're no' one o' them. This isn't ye," he pressed.

After Emily had placated the crew with the rum, earning their accolades, and ordered them to help with the captain's injuries, and they'd listened, she almost felt like she belonged. She'd had their respect. The crew trusted her with the captain's wellbeing. She kind of was...one of them.

Captain Lemoine had agreed to allow her back on the ship, even after knowing the truth. If he could accept her, could everyone else? That meant she had a chance to stay with the pirate crew, live the adventurous life of her silly dreams.

They weren't so silly anymore.

But could she truly be happy, knowing she could never be with the captain? It was just her luck the one man she believed was perfect happened to be gay.

Was Fergus's surprising offer the best she'd ever get? Or should she take her chances on the ship and retrieve her necklace?

Fergus leaned in close and flicked his head toward the room behind them. He whispered, "Does he know?"

If Emily told him the truth, Fergus could tell the whole crew, and she'd have to flee for her life, preventing her from stepping foot on the ship. Even worse, the captain's wasn't in a position to escape. His punishment would be severe. Emily had to lie. "He doesn't."

"Well, I should've suspected, as yer still standing here. In which case, it's no' too late." Fergus rose to his full height, and Emily tipped her face up to meet his gaze. "Emile,"—he paused, knowingly—"Due tae our unfortunate location, I canny retain th'approval o' my kin, and likewise, yers. But I'll stay here, a farmhand or fisherman, if it means I can have yer hand in marriage." Fergus held out his open palm, offering her a hammered metal ring with two hands holding a single heart.

A proposal? Emily had to remember marriages were more for business than love in these days, so she shouldn't have been surprised. But she still couldn't take Fergus seriously.

Emily touched Fergus's forearm to let him down gently. "I can't stay here with you. My only way home is back on that ship. You must understand."

Fergus stared her down, a thin line forming his mouth. "Canny I make myself more plain? Staying wi' them means yer death. Staying wi' me is a humble an' honest life. Can ye really choose *them*?" He was flabbergasted, not heartbroken.

Emily removed her hand from his arm. Captain Lemoine was her only means to the end she sought. If she couldn't have him—she clearly couldn't—Emily needed to get home. Her friends would miss her, and she'd be fired soon. Then unpaid bills would pile up all over again. She didn't want to slide back into the vicious cycle of collection notices, garnishments, and eviction. It was incredibly difficult to break that cycle and begin to save for another attempt at changing her life. Emily must get home before the life she knew was over.

"I am going with them," Emily said softly.

Fergus's back stiffened. His upper lip curled. "Ye're choosing a motley group o' murderers an' thieves. All they search fur is treasure. All they want is money! I thought ye were better than that. I was wrong."

Emily frowned. That couldn't be right. Emily witnessed them taking cargo to help fund their operations—saving men from brutal merchant captains. To avoid capture or destruction by the Royal Navy, they'd dumped all the cargo. In that case, saving her and Fergus earned them nothing. Fergus should be grateful. Emily was. The pirates had been nothing like Fergus's Captain Sinclair.

"I don't believe you."

Fergus's eyes softened. "Ye're making a mistake, but if ye change yer mind before the *Sea Lion* sails, find me. I'll be waiting." With that, Fergus pocketed the ring, and he descended the stairs and walked straight out the front door.

Emily turned around and startled at the eavesdropper. Captain Lemoine stood in the doorway, one arm across his middle, supporting his broken ribs. Admiration curved his lips.

"It's rude to listen to other people's conversations, and you should be sleeping."

The captain hooked his finger at her, urging her near.

Concerned, Emily rushed to his side and lifted his arm over her shoulders. "Is everything okay? Are you bleeding? Hurting? I have a couple pills left if you need one."

"Assist me back inside."

Emily frowned and moved them both back into the room. "You shouldn't have stepped out on your own."

The captain shifted his footing and flinched.

"You need more pain relief." Emily attempted to hunt down her ibuprofen in her pouch one-handedly.

The captain captured her chin with his fingers, stopping her. "You chose us."

"Of course I did. We have a mutual agreement, and I don't break promises."

"Before we return to the ship, separated not geographically, but in all the ways that matter, I need you to kiss me," Captain Lemoine said softly. "Even if it's for the last time."

Emily tilted her head, completely puzzled. "What? I thought you... You know, preferred men."

Captain Lemoine smiled. His thumb brushed against her jaw. "I prefer you. And if I can only have you for a day, so be it. I'd always chose a lifetime of pining over losing you, instead of bearing the unrequited ache in my heart. Kiss me."

"Unrequited?" Emily asked softly. He thought she didn't feel that way about him.

"Kiss me, please. I'll beg you until the very last moment."

He didn't have to beg. Emily's lips found his, carefully, gently exploring without injuring the captain further. Her hands moved into his long hair, so silky, and she melted against his chest. Those thick arms she'd waited for wrapped around her, holding her close, desperate to never let go. The world fell away. He still wanted her, and Emily wanted him, too.

Hope filled her chest with warmth, and she gripped it like a lifeline.

Chapter 18

A POUNDING ON THE motel room door stirred Emily awake. The captain dozed peacefully next to her, the lines of his face soft, and Emily brushed a lock of wavy brown hair from his eyes. He'd told her everything she wanted to hear, and Emily couldn't wait to explore the new man in her life. Except they had an expiration date the minute they stepped foot onto the *Sea Lion*. The rapping continued.

"Just a minute." Emily swung her legs off the bed and checked her man-like appearance. She tucked her blonde hair back under her red kerchief, even though most of the men had longer hair than her.

Emily opened the door to find the muscle-bound Cantu frowning. That couldn't be good news.

"Can I help you?"

"Emile, we're all grateful you saved the captain."

Emily didn't believe the man knocked just to show appreciation, when he could be doing any number of activities conducive to arriving at port. Still, she smiled. "It was nothing. I couldn't have done it without your help."

"I beg to differ, sir. Your knowledgeable skills and quick action saved him. Don't know how we'd continue the account without him. He's the one with the amazing plan, and because of that, I've been sent on behalf of

Quartermaster Price. Where is the captain?" Cantu leaned around her shoulder to check the bed.

Emily didn't move out of the way. "He's sleeping."

"Rouse the captain at once. We have a problem he must address."

Emily didn't want to. His stitches needed rest, but Cantu had a concerning look of worry on his face. "One moment."

While the beefy Cantu waited in the doorway, Emily woke the captain. His eyelids fluttered open, and he smiled. His palm lifted to cup her cheek, but Emily intercepted, gripping his hand in hers as if supporting him to stand. Before he could comment on her blocking move, she said, "Price needs you."

The lines on his face returned, and Captain Lemoine found Cantu in the doorway. He nodded his acknowledgement, and the messenger left. "I much prefer spending our only day with you in my bed, but duty calls, I'm afraid."

Emily helped him to his feet, and he groaned and flinched. On his feet, Captain Lemoine held out his arm, urging her closer. Emily melded to his side like a steel structure supporting a wind damaged skyscraper.

Captain Lemoine gazed at the open door and exhaled. "Ready, doctor?"

Emily shuffled him out of the room and down the stairs meticulously. At the round table where the crew had entertained themselves the night before, Price, Boatswain Karl, Cantu, and the other officers of the ship waited. Emily eased the captain onto the last empty chair and stood behind him.

THE ACHES IN HIS ribs always eased with Emile at his side, and Lemoine was floating on clouds that she'd felt the same way about him. Alas, their day had to be spoiled. Staring at the grave faces before him, the pain spiked.

Quartermaster Price said, "As you know, dumping our hold to evade the Royal Navy has cost us. With nothing to sell and dismal funds left, our spending needed to be wise. So, I ordered the crew to stock up on supplies."

"Then what problem has urged my rousing?" the captain asked, frustrated at the disturbance to his sleep for nothing.

Price leaned forward. "We can't afford enough provisions for the whole crew to sail to Florida and back. Foregoing either is not wise, as you know."

That was a problem. The crew knew of the prize they were after. Asking for volunteers to give up what amounted to riches was simply not going to be accepted. "What of our credit on the house?"

"Used."

Emile asked from behind his chair, "I don't understand what's wrong."

Price said, "We need a guaranteed prize of meat...and rum...on our journey, or we must cut the number of hands continuing this account."

Emile cleared her throat and asked, "I don't see how anyone should be removed from the ship. So, how can we guarantee a prize?"

Price patiently explained to the new recruit, "There's a rumor of a goat supply ship sailing this way in a few days' time. If we can reach it first and take it successfully, then we'll have no problem."

"That's a lot of speculation," Emile said. She was right, but the officers glared at her. "What?"

At that, his officers turned to him for the decision. Captain Lemoine made a non-promise to keep Emile by his side so he could return her necklace. That jewel was rightfully owed to the crew. Its sale would solve this problem entirely. Not only would Emile never forgive him for such a betrayal, but the crew would punish him for defrauding the company of such a prize, punishable by marooning. As Emile's secrets had risked her life, so had his own. Lemoine said to the officers, "We lay out the situation for the crew, let them decide whether to continue the account."

"What does that mean?" Emily asked.

"Vote," Price said. "We need a minimum number of hands to overtake a prize and sail after an expected number of injuries. But if too few men volunteer, I'll choose who goes."

"Emile, how are the captain's injuries healing?" Price asked.

Lemoine didn't appreciate the slight. "I am at liberty of answering about my own condition."

Price countered, "A sound judgment; however, sir, you are not a doctor."

"Emile," Lemoine said. "You found broken ribs?"

Emile nodded. "As best as I can figure without proper equipment. I didn't want to palpate and make things worse. It's best to assume so for better healing."

The strange woman, traveling alone with another woman who carried chocolate and a jewel of great value, clearly had a fantastic education. How could he reconcile her appearing to have a privileged upbringing with the tale of her father abandoning her to poverty? That was the missing piece of the Emile puzzle.

Lemoine added to Emile's assessment. "I deal with recurring spikes of pain, but mostly a dull ache. I can function with assistance."

"Excellent. We hold the vote at noon. Spread the word." Price collected his cocked hat and strolled out. The officers followed, and at the doorway, they split into pairs to track down the rest of the crew. No easy feat when the men were granted shore leave.

There was a gentle murmur of patrons filling the tables for lunch. The clatter of dishware came from nearby as the lovely ladies served the orders. The scent of food wafted over. Lemoine had dined on hardtack and diluted wine near the end there. They'd come too close on their provisions. He needed to order Emile a proper meal.

Emile took his hand in hers and leaned closer. "Now that they're gone, can you tell me how you really feel?"

Lemoine didn't want her to worry. "Having you at my side lessens the pain. I told the truth." He smiled reassuringly. "Now, you must be fatigued from so much exertion and only tack to fuel you. As I require your further assistance, I need you to be strong and healthy. So, let us partake in The Golden Macaw's finest offerings on the island."

Emile nodded, and Lemoine was proud to feed her. He ordered a meal for them, but when the dishes emerged, Emile tilted her head. "What is it?"

Lemoine couldn't wait for this. Everything Emile saw and heard brought more puzzle pieces to life.

"I recognize the wine and grapes, but I don't know what this is."

Lemoine smiled and pointed. "That is turtle and this is fish."

Emile smiled. "I'm always down for something new. Thank you so much. I'm starving."

"It's not a gesture worthy of merit." The captain minimized her appreciation. Seeing her satisfied was enough for him.

"To me it is. You understand I have no way of repaying you?"

That necklace in his possession... "Do not worry yourself over it."

Emile lifted a forkful of succulent turtle to her lips, and she closed her eyes over the tender meat. A murmur came from her throat. She grinned. "It's beefy. Is it always like this?"

"The method of preparation does differ from one establishment to another."

"I mean life here, scraping by for food. Not knowing if the people around you are trustworthy, and at any second everything you've built could come crashing down. Oh, and the Royal Navy always seeking your head. It seems like a very stressful life."

Where would Emile get an idea like that? "My head?"

"I just meant in general."

"What you describe might sound stressful, but it's better than the alternative." The captain swallowed a generous gulp of wine, taking the edge off the ache from his ribs to his thigh.

Emile popped a grape into her mouth. "What alternative is worse than a noose?"

"I could think of many things."

"Such as?"

Emile wasn't giving this up. Lemoine wasn't sure what the woman was after, but since they only had the day together, there was not much use to bleeding for her. "Not having a home to return to."

Emile's eyes fell to her plate. "Your home? Are you from somewhere around France?"

Captain Lemoine grinned. "Did my accent give it away or my stunning good looks?"

Emile laughed, a harmonious sound that brought a smile to his heart.

The captain wiped his mouth on a cloth napkin and gave her the story. "King Louis the fourteenth revoked the Edict of Nantes in 1685. I'm sure you've heard about it. My grandparents refused to convert their religion, and they brought my parents and me across the ocean. At ten years of age, I found a new life in the French colonies, but I do miss the French countryside."

"What brought you out here to Nassau?"

"It's a long story, but pursuing finer things steered me from the plantation to the sea, and now I'm here to rectify that mistake, no matter how long it takes."

And the necklace would've gotten Lemoine off the ship at once. But the crew would've hunted him down for turning his back on them. He had to push forward. He had to claim as much treasure as he could find before it was too late. And after discovering Emile's poor upbringing, he was thrilled she'd earn a share just for being by his side.

She deserved the finer things in life, too.

19

Chapter 19

Sweaty men, calmer after a night of release on shore, crowded on the main deck and around the rail, bringing the scent musky man with them. Instead of whatever debauchery they'd engaged in, they should've made time for a bath.

The blinding noon sun had Emily squinting at the quartermaster during his speech. Being from the frozen north, she'd never wished for cloudy days, but today, the endless reflective light of the Caribbean Sea had her wishing for sunglasses. Too bad none of the vendors the captain had showed her carried eyewear.

She did get to pet a goat, though.

Despite the rules of her and the captain pretending like there was nothing between them, she stayed by his side like a good doctor. Emily wasn't just supporting his weight. She leaned into him, relishing in the touch. So far, he'd kept his word to keep her secret...*their* secret, but the chaos of the impending vote meant Captain Lemoine hadn't returned her necklace yet. They had time.

"We have sufficient provisions for forty men, no more. Show of hands who wish to continue the account toward Florida." Hands raised in the air, and Price wrote on his clipboard.

Men discussed it among themselves, and one man asked, "Spain will be there for the recovery, no?"

"It is presumed, yes," Price said.

Several men whispered to each other, and left in pairs and threes. Emily picked up some mumbles about not enough prizes lately to take on that added risk.

Emily hadn't figured out what they were after in Florida. She imagined a series of barbarous merchant ships ripe for their crews to be freed, all conveniently docked together and loaded with goods to be confiscated and sold. The prospect of helping other new recruits adjust to their new freedom and life aboard a pirate ship excited her—more people she could almost relate to. "May I ask what the nature of this account is?"

Heads turned her way in surprise, as if she was dumb for not already knowing. Perhaps she was.

The quartermaster strolled over to her. He still wore a stick up his ass, but since he thanked her for her efforts and gave her a promotion, she softened against him. He had a tough job. Price focused on her, not at all annoyed by the interruption. "A Spanish treasure galleon awaits us off the coast of Florida. As word spread, several ships have set sail to claim a fortune for their crew. We must move quickly."

The remaining men cheered. Confused, Emily caught a glance at the captain, whose face was impassive. "Is that all?"

"Is that all?" the quartermaster repeated in disbelief. "A fortune, at the expense of an enemy nation, is not good enough, Porter? What a strange man you are."

The crew laughed.

Emily wasn't. "You're planning to steal money from a foreign government? I thought you people rescued merchant crews." Emily turned to the captain for an answer, but he only looked at her, unflinching, unapologetic. Had Fergus been right this whole time?

Quartermaster Price squinted into the sunlight at her. "I understand you're new on this crew, and somehow confused about seafaring life. We have no ownership paying us wages. As the captain had explained when you signed, we all work together for a fair share of the earnings."

"Earnings from what work? Because it sounds like you aren't in the business of rescuing sailors from nasty captains and compensating yourselves with their trade goods."

Price tilted his head in utter confusion. The corners of his lips lifted in amusement—the first time Emily had seen such humor on his otherwise attractive face. "The Crown steals from everyone. We only seek to even the playing field, but we aren't greedy. Once we're rich, we'll depart each other's company. None of us wants to hang at the gallows of Williamsburg."

Wanting to be rich *wasn't* greedy?

"Now, if I've explained the situation clear enough for you"—the crew chuckled, and Emily frowned—"then we'll commence the vote."

At Price's question, hands went up, but not Emily's. How could she join this pack of greedy thieves and murderers? She wasn't one of them—the signature she'd signed wasn't her name.

"Emile, raise your hand so the quartermaster can count you," the captain urged quietly.

"No," Emily hissed back. "I'm not joining you. I'm not like you, and I don't want to be part of this monstrous, barbaric...thing...you have here."

The crew closed in around her, not with the excitement for the announcement of rum, but the darkness of an insult. Captain Lemoine sent her a warning glare, but Emily didn't care. Fergus was right. These people were despicable, and it was about time someone made it clear to them. "You're all selfish bastards. What is wrong with you? Why can't you get regular jobs and stop stealing from people? How would you feel if everything you worked for was taken from you, just because an opportunist wanted it? Put yourself in their shoes. You'd hate it, just as I did."

The captain gripped her upper arm and said to the quartermaster, "He stays. Count him in."

Price nodded.

With restrained fury, Captain Lemoine pulled her through the crowd and into his private cabin, panting and gasping with pain. He locked the door behind them and leaned against it, sweating with the exertion. "You promised to help heal me."

Emily's anger kept pouring out. "And you shouldn't be moving like that. You're going to tear your stitches or crack your ribs worse, and I can't do anything for your ribs. Do you want a punctured lung? Because that's how you get a punctured lung." She didn't know if that was true or not, but it sounded good.

The captain approached her and shoved her to the bed. Beads of sweat trickled down his forehead. The captain's voice sounded like gravel with restrained anger. "There is much you need to learn before you end up causing both our deaths."

Emily reeled. In the spirit of the moment, the angering betrayal of the truth, she'd forgotten her outburst could lead directly to the crew murdering them both—and rightly so. "Then talk fast." Because she was five seconds from trashing this cabin, until she found her necklace, and leaving.

Captain Lemoine paced, despite the pain clear on his features. Emily wanted to comment, but she let him talk. "You don't know any of their stories, where they came from, why they chose this life—not even mine! Yet you presume to know them all and judge them to be unworthy."

He was right, Emily thought, anger deflating. But that didn't ease the pain she felt.

"If any of them had been born to a privilege of earning livable wages, we wouldn't be here."

A single word caught Emily's attention. "We?" Emily had remembered his words—pursuing finer things steered him from the plantation to the sea. Did a plantation not pay fair wages? Were those 'finer things' just greed, and Emily's heart had missed that meaning?

The captain paced the room with a hand on his stitched hip for support.

Emily pleaded, "Please sit down before you make the injuries worse." There was condescension in her voice, but with all the adrenaline coursing through her system, she couldn't help it, even though the words were sincere.

The captain sank onto his mattress next to her and swiped at his brow. "Half of those men are freed slaves."

Emily's brows popped. She had no idea.

"Another fifteen are from merchant ships with tyrant captains, like you."

That was familiar.

"And the rest followed the call of the sea when the land was disappointing."

"Which category do you fit in?" Emily asked softly.

"I can be categorized by two of those groups. After the religious unrest I told you about, our family boarded a slave ship headed for the French colony, Saint-Domingue, in Hispaniola. Have you heard of it?"

Emily nodded, the modern Haiti.

He continued, "All of us children worked on the sugar plantation, but the plantation owner's daughter caught my wandering eye. Our quick romps during the evenings led me to proposing a marriage of love, but her father denied the pairing, citing my station as unworthy of her."

Emily cringed. That was probably a word that stung him personally.

"After that, I watched her each day—so close, but so far away—and it pained me, until one day I took to the sea. I signed onto a merchant crew, transporting sugar. Unfortunately, I didn't understand how poor the wages were."

The urge to rest a hand on his thigh in comfort distracted her. What could she say to that? The man was a romantic at heart.

"You insist on understanding why I shot Captain Sinclair before burning and sinking his ship."

Emily nodded, afraid of interrupting, but encouraging him to continue.

"My merchant captain was an abusive man, an equal to Sinclair. You saw those scars exposed during my whipping?"

Emily did. They were alarming in their numbers and depth.

"My merchant captain punished me several times, because I attempted to right the wrongs on board."

"But why transfer the abuse onto another man?"

Captain Lemoine smiled and looked at the floor. "Not everyone believes as you and me. Donald Sinclair had been my equal aboard the sugar merchant ship. He'd always been a nasty fellow, supporting our captain's devious ways. Cheering his punishments and figuring inventive new ones. I'd always known Sinclair would turn out like him."

Emily's mouth opened. "I had no idea."

"Admitting you were abused by an equal isn't information you want freely floating around. For a pirate, it could mean a merchant wants retribution, and that's devastating to everyone."

Emily finally understood, even though she'd never seen a true fight.

"When our merchant ship was taken by a pirate ship, it was Captain Hornigold and the *Marianne* who granted us freedom. Last I'd heard, he's still capturing prizes around the Caribbean and adding to his flotilla."

Emily blinked and sucked in a breath. *The* legendary Captain Hornigold? Emily had to stop herself from asking if Lemoine had his autograph. A light feeling overcame her, and she inhaled deeply to center herself.

"Is something the matter? You look as if you've seen a ghost."

"I...I just might have." Emily shook out her hands and exhaled several deep breaths to calm herself, but it wasn't working. Actual, real history was here. All around her. So many people she could meet. So many hands she could shake. So many questions. The fangirling was back.

"Well then, Shall I dispatch these upsetting apparitions before we set sail?"

Emily chuckled. "Not necessary." She replayed the captain's words in her mind. "Pirate Captain Benjamin Hornigold had rescued your crew. What happened to your captain? Was he tied up, shot, and blown to pieces?" The specific punishment would make ironic sense.

"Captain Hornigold's first mate, Edward Teach, shot him before sinking the ship. I continued the tradition of freeing tormented crews while on the account."

Emily grinned. "Blackbeard? You're talking about Blackbeard?" She couldn't believe it.

"For not knowing anything of sea life, you appear well-versed in people." Captain Lemoine squinted at her in playful suspicion.

"I have one more question." Actually, a million, but that would only lead to more questions on the captain's side, and she still needed to avoid those. "What did the crew mean when they said you only gave them 'failure after failure'?"

Captain Lemoine shook his head. "Many of the sailors were upset about the prizes being lower than they had been. Too long at sea wears on a man. But if you mean Hooper—if he doesn't get a pint of rum every night, he deems the day's work a failure. Too many in a row makes him want to mutiny, and he riled up everyone else. Loud mouth, that one."

"If it's so common, why *doesn't* he mutiny?" Emily thought on her words. "No offense, or anything. I think you're a great captain."

Captain Lemoine grinned at her compliment. "Hooper knows he can't lead. But he's mighty good at complaining. Now that you understand our situation, will you come peacefully on the recovery mission?"

"Recovery?" Emily was confused all over again. "I thought you're going after a Spanish treasure ship, which sounds...unwise, honestly."

"A hurricane felled the treasure galleon. She rests under the sea, with gold spread all over. Since the Spaniards have not the resources to chase away all opportunity seekers, whoever brings up gold and escapes keeps it. I want every man on this crew to capture their share of nature's happenstance, and walk away to live their lives."

Less thieving and murdering, and more like finders keepers. In some situations, she could get behind that. And a wealthy foreign government that stole from indigenous cultures all along Central and South America was okay to her. Ideally, it would be returned, but that wasn't feasible. "I'll stay."

The captain beamed and moved to kiss her, but he stopped himself. "I've survived torture, abuse, starvation, the threat of mutiny—actual threat by prior crews, and never once have I endured something this difficult."

Emily apparently didn't have the whole story. "What's so difficult?"

"Keeping my hands off you. I'm beyond delighted you're here now."

The captain told her everything. Nothing more from him stood between them. He was just as amazing as she'd thought. Did Emily trust him enough to tell her secret? Would he accept it? If they weren't going to stay together, it didn't matter. But could they?

She'd have to stay here, and figure out new skills and live without all the creature comforts she'd always known. Or the captain joined her in the twenty-first century. How would that work? He didn't have papers. He couldn't get a job or manage finances. He could learn, just like her, but the curve was much steeper in her world. There was so much to think about, Emily didn't know where to start.

Or if any of it was possible at all.

Chapter 20

EMILY AND THE CAPTAIN returned to the deck while the vote continued. The crew shifted their weight, frowning and gesturing, and the occasional outburst of disagreement startled her. The vote wasn't going well. Too many men weren't willing to go.

The captain frowned at the sight.

Emily held tight to his side as they approached Price.

"What's the status?" Captain Lemoine asked.

"The crew has been reduced by many," Quartermaster Price said. "But not enough. I need to start choosing who goes. Officers are all staying, including you, Doctor Porter."

Doctor Porter sounded so weird. Emily brushed it away though.

"And we have provisions enough for the remainders?" Captain Lemoine asked.

"If I can get ten more volunteers to go, we'll be set to sail."

The extended crew renegotiations didn't need her or the captain. Price was fully competent. Emily wanted a minute to rest herself. "I'm going to have a seat. Join me?"

"I must stay here with Price. Go ahead." The captain swung his arm off her shoulders.

Emily stepped away, watching him for signs of distress. Satisfied with his composure, she stretched her aching neck and back and wove her way to the bulwark. Emily hopped up onto the rail, watching the remaining activities unfold. Through the crowd, a twiggy man approached, and Emily stiffened. "Fergus, what are you doing here? You left. You're free, just like you wanted."

"Being free disny seem as important when th'one person I want is trapped here, surrounded by murderers an' thieves. Who else is going tae keep ye safe?"

Emily frowned and read between the lines. "You signed the articles for me? But that's against everything you believe in."

Fergus leaned in close. "Aye, an' it was difficult, as Price is trying tae cut sailors fur the account. I thought o' what ye said. Th'risk is oot there. Whether I be oan th'merchant side awaiting th'pirates or th'pirate side awaiting th'noose. Then th'choise was plain."

Emily whispered, "You can't tell anyone about me, or they'll kill me."

He whispered in her ear, "I know, but I'm here tae protect ye, not hurt ye."

Emily didn't like a stranger having her life in his figurative hands. Mouth hanging open, she watched Fergus sink back into the sea of bodies. A longboat full of volunteers waited to be lowered to the water.

"McNeel, Abbas, Hazelip, Kanumba, you're off," Quartermaster Price ordered. Groans and whines came from the crowd as the chosen men wove their way toward the waiting longboat. "And that's it. Anchor's up in two hours."

The quartermaster closed his book and retreated to his private room below deck. The crew dispersed to their stations. Apparently, it took that long to lift the anchor. Men fitted the capstan with their levers and heaved around the axis point, singing a merry shanty to coordinate the rhythm of their movements. Others below deck must be working the messenger cable, a tedious process of attaching and detaching a separate rope to help lift the anchor.

Emily didn't see which way Fergus went, and she hoped to avoid him entirely. Just the idea that he wanted to marry her gave her the worst creeps. She didn't even know the guy. Him keeping her secret the whole while and disappearing after the account was finished was a best-case scenario.

The captain limped over toward her, and Emily rushed to his side and gathered him into her arms, intercepting his attempt at independence. Together, under the shadow of the cabin, they watched the crew set sail, a practiced dance of teamwork, shouted commands, and the rustling of canvas and sliding of lines through pulleys. All she could think about was the captain, an all-consuming entity who was strapped to her side and quickly invading her heart. Now was the perfect time to ask for the necklace, but she didn't want to disturb this peace between them. Not yet.

"How are the stitches feeling?"

The captain shrugged. "Enough rum and nothing is bothersome."

Emily couldn't argue with that, but they'd already struggled with the rum quantity, and the last thing she needed was another riot on her hands. Speaking of which, "Do we have enough rum on board to keep the masses content?"

"I wager Price has that settled. I must be off to chart the course to Florida's coast. Check on my person whenever you see fit." The captain winked at her and retreated to the navigation room behind them.

Emily glanced around for witnesses, but everyone was preoccupied preparing the ship. Alone on the deck, Emily climbed up onto roped cargo to enjoy a beautiful view without worrying about the waves tossing her overboard. A beautiful land, a barbarous time, and instead of reading about it in the books, she was here now. If Tyler could see her, would he laugh and say it suits her or would he tell her to grow up...again? Emily brushed him out of her thoughts and inhaled the soft sea air. She hoped wherever her friends were sent, they were having a relaxing and safe vacation.

A group of men came out to the deck, and with nothing pressing to do, Emily watched them. Fergus was in the mix, but so far, he stayed busy. A pair of the men leaned over the rail on the opposite side of the ship from her and called down. They hoisted up a longboat full of men and the last of the supplies. With a wooden crate in his hands, Fergus broke away from the group and approached her.

"Have ye retrieved yer necklace yet?" he asked.

"Not yet. Why?"

Fergus hopped up onto the cargo next to her and rested the crate in his lap. "I saw it. Th'captain took it oot o' his pocket an' closed it inside a box in the hold."

A surge of excitement tore through her. "You're certain?"

Fergus nodded with a smile.

"Which one? Where?"

Fergus chuckled. "I have a plan. Just stay close."

Emily was thrilled to have someone willing to help her out. She followed Fergus across the deck and down the ladder, but someone was blocking the entrance to the hold—a security guard. Hooper, the man who conspired against the captain over rum but without the guts to follow through.

"What business you have here?" Hooper demanded, arms crossing over his broad chest, hopped up on his new authority.

"Last o' th'supplies are here." Fergus lifted the crate to prove his story true. "Price sent us tae check on th'rum supply tae make sure we have enough before we set sail."

Emily believed it was a lie, but she would take any help she could get.

"Is that so?" Hooper scrutinized them both, including the crate in Fergus's arms. "Anchor's already up. Price wouldn't send anyone back now."

"It's th'truth o' it, an' Florida's a long way off," Fergus said, and Hooper stepped aside. Fergus rushed her through the door and closed it behind them, having only candlelight to work with.

"Which one is it?" Emily asked, scanning for the likeliest contender, but her eyes hadn't adjusted yet. Fergus set down the crate in his hands, and Emily added, "What did it look like?"

While squinting at the barrels and shifting around crates, now much more full than last time she'd dug through here, the door behind her swung back open. Fergus approached Hooper and talked to him quietly. A frown on the guard's face set Emily on edge. Whatever just happened wasn't good.

"Come with me now, Porter." Hooper reached for her.

Emily tilted back out of the larger man's grasp. "What's this about? Price sent us, right, Fergus?" All the friendliness was gone from her friend's face and at once, Emily knew she'd made a grave mistake.

"He forced me tae help him enter th'hold." Fergus pointed at Emily like a child proclaiming the guilty party. "I'm innocent in this conspiracy. Just ask Price; he'll know naught o' this. It's all Porter's doing."

Fergus's word vomit to Hooper had Emily's stomach churning, and her avalanche of questions would only make her sound guilty. Emily said nothing, allowing Hooper to haul her to the aft of the gun deck. "This isn't right," Emily tried explaining as he dragged her along. "I only want what's best for the crew. You know that."

They ducked and swerved through the tightly packed narrow pathways. "That's not my decision to make, now is it?"

Up on the gun deck, rectangles of light dotted the floorboards alongside each cannon through the open gun ports, airing out the ripe scent of unbathed men. Their footsteps creaked against the hardwood, and gulls cawed nearby. If it weren't for the inhabitants of the ship, this would be the best vacation she'd ever had. Instead, Hooper stopped them at the quartermaster's cabin and knocked.

Price verbalized their permission to enter, and Hooper's firm hand forced her inside and explained what he'd caught her doing, focusing solely on Fergus's side of the story. Price nodded with a grim set to his mouth, and Hooper shut the door behind her on his way out, preventing her escape. Alone with the quartermaster, Emily crossed her arms protectively over her chest.

The quartermaster stood and strolled around his desk. "The captain had already taken your punishment for the last attempt to pilfer from the hold. Seems I was right to set a guard upon the door. Because of your position, I'll allow you a chance to defend yourself."

There was so much wrong with that, but Emily crafted a fib to lean into Price's reasonable side. "I needed to be sure there were enough medical supplies before we left. No one wants to be caught in a battle without the proper equipment to fix wounds." The humid dampness gave her a chill.

"When the mouse was caught creeping into the grain, the reason of a meal was excused once and warned against. When the mouse failed to heed that warning, and the cat held the mouse's tail did the story change. So which is the truth? The mouse's story before or after pressure was applied? The reason mattered not. The story mattered not. Words were meaningless when they didn't match the actions. The mouse's decision to disobey orders demanded consequences."

That was an eloquent way of saying Emily wasn't get out of a punishment this time. The question was the magnitude of it. "I'm the mouse in this story?" Emily asked with disbelief, already knowing the answer. Fergus had planned this since he'd uncharacteristically decided to sign the articles. Why did her friend trick her?

"When the captain arrives, *he* shall serve your punishment." Price returned behind his desk with an air of finality.

A light knock on the door churned Emily's stomach. Price granted the visitor entrance, and when Emily met the captain's gaze, she silently pleaded for help and mercy.

"What's this all about?" the captain asked, limping closer, and shot Emily a fast glance of concern.

Hooper's smug smile at the door angered her, but it was closed on him once again.

Price said, "Porter was caught persuading another sailor to lie to the guard at the hold. What he sought, we don't know, but an attempt is still intent, and our doctor here was caught in the act. His theft is punishable by marooning."

The captain's features darkened with a contained rage that made Emily nervous. "This involves Fergus and Hooper, does it not? A man who incites protests with the intent to mutiny, and the other, who rejected the articles but returned, begging to be allowed aboard. I trust your judgment, Price, but how is that not suspicious?"

Emily was grateful the captain had her side...and saw reason. Yesterday she'd had their respect and admiration. Today they wanted to maroon her, leaving her to die. It was almost unbelievable how quickly their loyalties changed.

"Whether or not I believe them, the men wove their tale convincingly, and it will spread regardless of its truth," Price said calmly.

The captain tensed. "How can you trust those men over Porter?"

"The possibility of a thief among them is a direct threat to their trust, and right now, we need the crew united. The crew shall not stand for brushing another crime under the rug. So you see, my hands are tied."

The captain leaned on Price's desk, fury rolling off him. "I will not maroon our only doctor because of a story from Fergus and Hooper. This issue stays between us, and I'll warn Fergus and Hooper if their tongues wag once about this, they'll be the ones heaved over the starboard rail. Is that clear?"

The quartermaster's darkening features meant he didn't like his position challenged.

Emily piped in before things escalated beyond repair. "Price, you said yourself this crew owed me a debt. I want to cash it in to stay aboard the *Sea Lion*."

Price eyed her with a glimmer of respect, but his words were firm. "We do need a doctor, and it's too late to find another. We also need a competent captain moving into this account. Make no mistake—concessions shall not be given again. Don't worry about Fergus and Hooper. I'll take care of them. Get us to Florida."

The captain straightened, satisfied, and Emily followed him out the door. She shot a nasty glance at Hooper and tried to assist the captain's steps down the quiet gun deck, but he refused. Outside of earshot, Emily said, "What's wrong?"

Captain Lemoine didn't face her. Concerned, she reached out for his arm, but he tugged out of her grip.

"I have work to do," he snapped.

Emily stopped, dejected, and watched the captain limp up to the main deck. What had she done wrong this time?

Chapter 21

During their journey, the sky remained bright and clear, the waters calm. They had not encountered a goat supply ship, and Emily had overheard concerns the target had changed course, or some other ship got to her first. Either way, she was grateful only half the crew was on board, just so she didn't have to watch them fight to the death for the limited provisions they afforded.

Boatswain Karl assigned her to Fergus's side. Her friend had deliberately sabotaged her, and now there was an unspoken awkwardness between them, and every time he neared her, the hairs raised on her arms. She hated that a sliver of fear lingered. What had been Fergus's intent in nearly getting her marooned? It ate at her, but like the captain ordered, no tongues wagging about the ordeal.

Fergus showed her how to tie up the sails on the yardarm, and without any safety equipment, it was a harrowing but exhilarating experience. A fall to the deck or the water from that height would mean death after many broken bones. OSHA would have a field day on this ship.

For days, Emily watched the captain over her shoulder, catching glimpses here and there, but Captain Lemoine had refrained from glancing back, as if she'd hallucinated their whole forbidden relationship. No matter the legitimate concern she offered over his care, he'd refused her. The captain acted as if they'd never kissed or shared other very intimate moments, and that cut her deeply. If not for him, Emily had no reason to stay here. All day she secretly plotted her next attempt to find her necklace. She didn't believe it was left carelessly in the hold to be jettisoned the next time the Royal Navy appeared, or more likely, the Spanish Armada.

But first, the captain's diminished limp meant she needed to check his stitches, no matter his stubborn and likely inaccurate opinion of her. While cruising at a speed of about six knots and weather that allowed for more relaxed temperaments, Emily excused herself from Fergus and knocked on the navigation room door.

"COME IN," CAPTAIN LEMOINE called through the door. He'd been making adjustments to their course as the conditions changed, and in the middle of a calculation, he hadn't looked at his visitor.

He didn't want to hear any more from Price. Lemoine was already furious with himself, and throwing himself into his work was the only way to make things right. He had to get them to Florida swiftly and safely. The sooner they retrieved their gold, the sooner he could give Emile her just dues and bid her farewell with her necklace.

It was better that way, even if it hurt untold amounts.

The door closed, and Lemoine wrote down the final number. Satisfied, he looked up and frowned. Emile didn't belong in here, and her presence was risky. "I told you I don't need your aid any longer."

Emile stiffened, and Lemoine felt a pang of guilt. "I noticed your gait has improved. If you're healed, I need to remove your stitches."

Lemoine met her gaze and his anger softened. He wasn't upset with her. Only himself. He couldn't keep her safe. Any mistake from here on out would be her life, and likely his as well. But he could give up resistance for proper care. "Fair enough. This way."

Captain Lemoine stood and gestured for her to follow him into his cabin. When closed in together, remembering her naked in the bath, his breathing increased. Lemoine removed his tunic and untied his breeches slowly, trying to plead with himself this was only a medical visit to be over and done with.

It wasn't working well.

Emile approached cautiously, cheeks pinking with a beautiful flush. He liked that effect on her, and he loved that he caused it. Emile ducked, her fingers pressing gently around the area. "I don't feel any alarming heat, and the site is soft. Everything looks good here." Emile opened her pouch and removed a sewing kit. She slipped the mini scissors through her fingers. She leaned in close as she began the process of removing the stitches.

Something inside her pouch caught his eye. Lemoine pointed at her waist and asked, "What's that?"

"What's what?" Emile asked, focusing on her work.

"This." Unable to help his curiosity, Captain Lemoine slipped free the strange device and turned it over in his hands. It felt expensive, but he couldn't figure out why. The top of it was reflective, but not a mirror. And small holes on the sides were for inserting something, but Lemoine could never guess what. He'd never seen anything like it. "What does this do?"

Emile slipped it from his fingers as if it were fragile or dangerous. She looked at it, debating. "I'm afraid you wouldn't understand if I told you."

The captain made a snort of derision. Surely she didn't just insult him? "I've traveled the seas, Emile, for five and twenty years. Been to many countries the world over, and yet, you think me such a simpleton?"

Emile turned the black device over in her hands. "I can tell you, but this cannot change anything between us. For my safety and yours. Can we make that deal?"

Lemoine had many ideas of what could need such a disclaimer, and finally the last piece of the Emile puzzle was at hand. "Are you a spy? Is that why you're on the run? Is that why you won't tell me of your origins? Is that why you're so unfamiliar with our world out here at sea?"

Emile's lips lifted in mild humor. "Spy? No. My life isn't that exciting...wasn't...that exciting." She thought further and said slowly, "Remember when I said I came from an island off the coast of the colonies? It's not true. I couldn't explain—in a way you'd understand, in a way anyone from here would understand. See, even where I'm from, the explanation of my home makes little sense. Do you understand?"

The captain blinked, trying to make heads or tails of it. "I'm not sure."

"It's not that I don't trust you with the truth; it's just...I don't want to be...I..." Emile trailed off.

"You can tell me, Emile. Whatever it is. Please tell me." He needed this trust from her. He wanted it dearly. If she could find it in her heart to open up to him, he could see a future with her.

Emile sighed. "I'm afraid of how you'll react."

Her declaration truly baffled him. "How could you be afraid of me? I've done nothing to cause you such unease. And if I have, my deepest apologies."

Tears shimmered on her lids. "Perhaps you should honor our previous deal. Return my necklace first."

The idea of making good on his word settled like a rock in his gut. Far from land, she couldn't escape with it. But knowing she had the option panged him. He knew he had to let her go, beyond this ship, back to her confusing home. But not yet.

Captain Lemoine still held onto a glimmer of hope. "Is that what you truly want?" A tear spilled over, and Lemoine brushed it carefully from her cheek with his thumb. "Why such tears, Emile?"

"I'm trusting you with the truth. I'm trusting you with my life. Remember that." Emile focused on the device, and it lit up like magic.

Lemoine frowned. Her fingers moved and after a few seconds, she turned the lighted side of the device to him. His eyes widened at an image so real, he had to touch it to be sure. No brush strokes were visible at all. How was it possible? The image was Emile, dressed in the most outlandish clothing he could imagine, smiling with her blonde hair down. And the next was her in the clothing she wore now with another woman, and both stood next to something shiny, metallic, and monstrous. Captain Lemoine couldn't begin to understand it.

Emile touched something and the image before him—the image in color!—changed again.

Lemoine backed up a step and fell onto the mattress. His hand moved to his forehead. "What is that? What...? How...?"

"These are pictures—photographs—of me out with friends. Everyday stuff. But that one was me and Angela in front of her car. This was us at the Tall Ships festival, where I was before appearing on Captain Sinclair's merchant ship. I didn't stow away." As she'd explained, her fingers moved the images back and forth...like magic.

Captain Lemoine didn't know what to believe. "Magic transported you here. You're a witch?"

Emile waved her hands to brush those words away. "No, not at all, no. Witches don't exist, but apparently time travel does."

Captain Lemoine considered the concept hogwash. Looking at the proof before him, he had been a simpleton, and his respect and fear grew.

"I'm from Wisconsin, a state in the United States of America, which doesn't exist yet. I was at a festival enjoying the ships of the past with vendors selling beer, food, and crafts." Emile swiped the device again, showing him while explaining.

Captain Lemoine was frozen in terror and fascination.

"My friend and I bought necklaces at a vendor. When we boarded the tourist ship, a barque, by the way, the guide ordered us to take them off the ship. Angela and I opted to wear them instead, and when I put mine on, the next thing

I knew, I was here in the past. I don't know what happened to Angela. I have no other explanation, but I assure you, this is the truth."

As much as he didn't understand it, he believed it. "You'd told me if you got your necklace back, you'd return home. That necklace is the only way," he said softly.

"It's only a theory, truthfully. For all I know, I'm stuck here. But if I put it on, over my head, it should take me home the same magical way it brought here me." Emile looked at the device again, fingers moving.

"This won't hurt you. It happened in my past—your future, okay? And I hope you take this in deeply, because my battery's almost dead." Emile sat next to him and held the device once again.

Captain Lemoine watched a man laughing and sloshing a red cup of liquid with his arm around...Emile, who also harbored a grin, but there was a sadness to her features.

"This was a party. We were celebrating Angela's birthday. That's Tyler."

Captain Lemoine stiffened. His mind blanked.

With a touch of Emile's magic finger, the moving pictures stopped. "I'm sorry, I just wanted to show you. This thing also makes phone calls to anyone in the world who also has one."

Lemoine shook his head and stood. He paced the room, ignoring the ache from his side. "Which would be no one."

"As long as I'm the only one from the future with a cell phone, that's true. Although, without cell towers, it doesn't matter, anyway."

Ignoring her nonsensical words, the captain continued pacing the cabin. The answers he sought made no sense, but at the same time made perfect sense. It explained why she understood nothing of their world, but yet marveled over ordinary people—Hornigold and Blackbeard. She knew who they were from stories. Lemoine noted she hadn't heard of him, and he didn't know whether to be concerned or not.

It also explained how she could appear to be privileged with her clothing, smooth hands, and straight white teeth, while claiming a childhood of poverty. His world, what he knew, wasn't her world.

Emile slipped the device back into her pouch and removed more chocolates. "Here." She offered him a few. "These aren't rare or expensive where I'm from. And they aren't stolen." She emphasized the final two words.

He stopped and looked at her open palm. Unable to take from her, he closed her fingers over the candies. "They're rare and expensive here. Savor them while you still have them."

Emile frowned. "While I still have them?"

Captain Lemoine offered her a hand. She accepted, and he lifted her to her feet. "Kiss me."

"But the articles?" Emile said.

"Tell me one last thing. What is your name?"

Emile smiled. "Emily. Emily Porter."

"I'm certain Emily Porter didn't sign the articles." Captain Lemoine said, a sadness tugged at his heart. She didn't belong here at all, and there was nothing he could offer that would satisfy her. Not even all the gold in the wreck would be good enough. But he had to try. He wanted her to have all of it and return home to the life of privilege she deserved.

Emily chuckled. "She didn't."

"So kiss me, Emily," he whispered.

Her lips found his, and his arms found their way around her, pressing her close for the first time. His body felt hers. The shapes of a woman. He wanted his hands on her breasts, his mouth at the cleft between her thighs. He wanted his cock to explore regions that would have her calling his name in ecstasy. But so long as they were on this ship, as she'd explained, they couldn't.

Tears pricked his eyes. Despite knowing she needed to go home, he knew it would destroy him.

THE KISS HAD FELT like goodbye, and Emily memorized every movement, every taste of his lips she could.

Until an urgent knocking on the captain's door had him pull apart from her too quickly and too soon. With gruff irritation, he barked, "What's the matter?"

"Captain, sir, the location is in sight, but we're not alone."

Captain Lemoine turned to her. "I must go at once. I suspect we shall encounter hostilities. I *don't* promise to keep you safe."

Emily forced a smile and the promise of the non-promise. Unable to speak, she only nodded, and the captain rushed out the door, limping far less than he usually would.

Emily was alone. The captain bid her goodbye. He knew she had to return home, but he hadn't returned her necklace yet. She tried not to read further into that. He simply hadn't had a chance to since they'd made the deal.

Was it possible for her to stay here? Emily certainly wouldn't be happy minding a house while Captain Lemoine traversed the oceans, finding adventure, freeing merchant sailors, and collecting what he needed to keep themselves fed.

He was a pirate. He was a thief. Today he was collecting gold that was lost without harming anyone.

And he was an amazing man who was justified in his actions.

But could she join him here at sea, be a real pirate? Assuming the crew somehow accepted her as herself. Emily's job in the future was hardly sufficient to pay the rent. She'd dumped her thieving, disrespectful, gaslighting ex-boyfriend. Angela having put on her necklace meant she was gone, too. Her mother had passed away. Her father had vanished. She had just about nothing tying her to home.

Emily had the best adventure of her life in the last few weeks. And with a misty gaze at the captain's door, she no longer wanted to go, but knew she must. The crew—Hooper and Price especially—would never accept her. And Fergus would throw her under the bus in a heartbeat, because she'd rejected his proposal.

The vacation excitement of her trip through time would wear off soon, and she'd be missing her chocolate, hot showers, restaurants, safety standards of the future, grocery stores, online ordering, and even menstrual cups. She had bills, an apartment, and plants to water. Home was where she belonged.

Emily composed herself, double checked all her future stuff was tucked away, and exited to the main deck, hoping beyond hope they weren't going to be under fire again.

The captain stood on the quarterdeck above her with a spyglass pointing to the sea. Emily lifted a hand to shield the sun and gazed at the horizon. Several ships. Were they Royal Navy? Spanish Armada? Other pirates? Merchants on a detour?

Whoever they were, wouldn't be friendly.

Chapter 22

SEVERAL SHIPS DOTTED THE coastline, dancing along the fair weather waves. Emily didn't see a single Spanish banner among them. But the *Sea Lion* approached the starboard side of the nearest ship—a three-masted sloop with English emblems on the sails. Their ship had communicated a willingness to converse, and Emily watched them closely at the rail. The Englishmen aboard the sloop leaned over the opposite rail, lifted their loot, and hauled full bags below deck like dutiful ants, one after the other. A man who appeared to be the captain of the sloop waved, and out of politeness, Emily waved back with a smile.

These weren't monsters, murders, or thieves. Just opportunists trying to change their stars without harming anyone. And Spain wasn't exactly innocent in how they'd commandeered this gold in the first place.

"Ahoy!" Captain Lemoine called over. "Seeking the lost gold, are you?"

"Aye!" the captain from the other side called back. "And we won't be giving any up! Find your own and be gone with you!"

Captain Lemoine gestured for the quartermaster to join him on the quarterdeck, and the men spoke in private. What syllables made their way over were blurred by the breeze. With a quick nod, Price moved through the crew, passing along the orders. All but the essential sailors dropped their current tasks and turned their attention to the sloop.

Emily had a sinking feeling something bad was about to happen, and her stomach knotted.

"This Spanish gold is free for the taking," Captain Lemoine called back. "If you'll not share either your loot or your successful location, then we shall stake our claim to this free territory!"

Emily accepted a recovery of lost gold, but this sounded like blatant thievery. How could he lie to her face? Emily glared at the back of the captain's head, wishing to see the hidden truth buried under his magnificent hair and fancy hat. But the *Sea Lion* crew, who were freeing pistols and cutlasses from their waistbands, drew her attention. Emily wasn't a fighter, and she didn't have arms. As the worry crossed her mind, a cutlass was pressed into her hand.

Fergus.

Emily frowned and tried to hand the weapon back. She didn't want his help, and she had no interest in touching something responsible for how many deaths already? "What are you doing? You already framed me for theft and almost got me marooned for it. I don't want to talk to you ever again."

"I didny ask ye tae say anything," Fergus smiled at this play on her words.

Emily only glared to make her point.

"But since ye mention it, I created that spectacle tae get ye removed from th'ship, so ye'd be safe from these people, from this"—he gestured to the sword in her hands. "But since ye were too stubborn tae accept th'way oot I offered, now ye must place yer fate in th'hands o' these ruffians an' murderers. As th'ship's de facto doctor, we'll defend ye as best we can, so get below deck fur yer own safety. I hope ye have a robust constitution."

Emily's anger deflated. He'd only tried to save her life in the only way he knew how. "Why didn't you just say something instead of tricking me?"

"Ye wouldn't have gone voluntarily."

No, no she supposed she wouldn't have. "And how would you have saved me from marooning? It's kind of a one-person punishment."

"I would've jumped in after ye."

A warm friendliness blossomed toward Fergus.

"Together we would've sailed away into the sunset, alive, safe, and free from men like these."

"Thank you." Whether for the sword or the attempt to save her life, she didn't know.

Fergus grinned and nodded. "When those men cross, I can only dae so much since our crew is half th'normal size. An' if ye fall, I am deeply sorry."

Fergus had far more experience with ship battles than she, so his flippant discussion around impending death startled her, as if it were expected. In all the times she'd gone camping, surrounded by bears, coyotes, foxes, raccoons, and other critters armed with teeth and claws, never once was she concerned for her life. In most places she camped, either she or her friends had spotty cell service at a minimum. Roads were easily traversable by city commuter car. The biggest risk to her life had been when she and Angela had rented a jet ski to drag an inflatable raft on the lake. Far from shore, Emily had jumped off the raft for a swim and Angela, after a few drinks, thought it'd be funny to drive away with it.

Emily was a great swimmer, but this impending battle was so much worse than anything she'd ever experienced. Emily was only a pirate in spirit. But instilling hope and building courage could have tremendous positive effects—neither of which Fergus had apparently heard of. "You're apologizing for my death when I'm not dead yet?"

Fergus double checked his pistol for shot and grasped it with a trembling hand. His grip on the cutlass was slightly firmer. "Aye. I fear it's an inevitability. I'm only a moderate swordsman myself. But if we both die, we die wi' honor in defending ourselves against th'worst scum o' the nation."

Emily didn't miss that irony. "And now you're one of them."

"Aye, it's true. Ye know how tae destroy a man's pride. Hold on tae yer britches, because here they come!"

Men swung over from the opposing ship with grunts and growls and frowns creasing their faces. Emily's heart perched itself in her throat as if seeking its own safety. She didn't have time to hide, but if she got caught deserting the crew in battle, that was punishable by marooning, too. No room for cowards on a pirate ship. Emily gripped the sword, sweaty hands trembling. She'd never killed anyone, as most civilized people hadn't, but she'd also never been cornered and fighting for her life. Despite her extensive camping experience, she'd never encountered a bear. And now she might not get to.

Swords clanged and crashed. Pistols fired. Clouds of gunpowder obscured the deck. The ship tilted with the waves, sending swords flying, missing their targets. Men shouted and grunted with their efforts, and Emily ducked and feebly swiped at nearby engaged foes while attempting to reach the ladder to the lower deck. She'd rather take her chances with bears and marooning. Or marooning with bears. This was suicide.

An English pirate stalked up to her with a grimace and a sword aimed to swipe, blocking her exit from the battle. Emily's hand trembled, and her grip tightened on the sword. She dug deep for an intimidating voice. "Back away. I don't want to hurt you." It most definitely wasn't scary at all.

The pirate closed in on her.

Emily's hands shook harder. "Please," she begged in a weak voice, tears threatening to spring free. Emily scanned for the captain, but she couldn't see him. What if he were already dead? Tears sprung to her eyes, but she blinked them away.

The enemy before her snorted with amusement. "What kind of pirate cries in battle? For your cowardice, you deserve death." The man spat and held his sword high for a devastating blow. But he stopped in his tracks, face slackening. The Englishman fell over like a tall sack of potatoes, and Fergus pulled his sword from the man's spine.

Her friend was smeared in blood, but he smiled in good spirits. "So far, we're alive."

Fear twisted Emily's face. How could he be so casual? Swords continued to clang and crash around them. Blood slicked the deck. With the captain's abrupt orders, they had no time to sand it. Bodies, some writhing in pain and others still as a stone, cluttered the slippery main deck. The fight spilled over onto the enemy ship. The men retrieving gold stopped to pick up a sword and defend their loot.

A pirate approached Fergus's back, and Emily pointed. "Watch out!"

Fergus turned with his sword ready to strike, but the enemy was quicker, splitting Fergus across the middle. Emily gasped. Her friend's face slackened, and he dropped to his knees and flopped onto his side. With a quick glance at his fatal wound, Emily knew there was nothing to be done. She stifled a scream. All Fergus ever wanted was to be free of this ship and take her with. He'd died for it, and it was her fault.

She'd known returning to the *Sea Lion* was a risk, but she never thought the threat could come from within. Lemoine ordered this attack, and now Fergus and many others were dead.

For money.

Wild-eyed and terrified, Emily held her cutlass up, wishing she'd taken a self-defense class. An English pirate swung his sword down, and Emily's crashed against his, the jolting impact almost making her drop it. He pressed harder, closer. She was no match for his strength, not by a long shot. He grinned with malicious pleasure as his sword brought her closer to the slippery and red-stained deck boards. If he hadn't been enjoying it so much, she would've been dead already.

Emily kneeled down to the floor, still holding the English pirate's sword at bay. He was playing with her, pressing only as hard as he needed to pin her down. What could she do before it was too late? Emily held her breath, struggling with the effort, on the verge of crying out to spare her life.

The pirate kneeled over her and lifted his sword for a final blow.

Emily saw her window. She kicked up at his crotch and sent him folding over. She scurried backward over the downed bodies and slick blood, smearing bodily fluids all over her outfit. The pirate's blade glinted with a slash through the air, but Emily moved her foot at the last second. Her arms shook with the force exerted to survive the attacker, and now a second one approached. Emily stood, wanting to run, but in every direction were small skirmishes of pirates on pirates, and even if she found a way through, she'd be sliced up by accident. This English pirate closed the distance, and Emily's insides turned to liquid. Surviving one was luck. She knew her odds against another were nil.

Less than nil.

THE SECOND ENGLISH PIRATE snarled and lifted his sword to strike. Emily moved her sword to protect her face, but her attacker paused, arm mid-air, and his head fell back. Her second attacker fell to the deck, and just as Fergus had before him, Captain Lemoine extracted his cutlass from the pirate's neck. Her captain held out his hand to her, and Emily smiled with relief. She was still pissed, but grateful to be alive.

"Are you well?" he asked.

Emily glanced at her blood-stained clothes and her friend's body. She doubted he was still alive. The crew of the *Sea Lion* had been far outnumbered. Emily was losing what small strand of hope she'd held onto. "I'm breathing. That's all I can say right now."

The pirate Emily had kicked in the crotch had returned to his feet and approached them both. Captain Lemoine swung at him, shifting the man's attention to himself. The captain's sword met the opponent's with grunts from his broken rib and a few slices on his arms. Emily could hardly watch as the men circled one another, feral rage of wild animals on their faces.

"Stop!" Emily shouted. She couldn't bear it any longer. The captain's head turned to her, and the pirate took the opportunity. Emily processed the movements in slow motion—the pirate's snarl turning to a smirk, the sword shifting position, the flickers of his arm muscles as he adjusted trajectory.

"Duck!" Emily shouted before the pirate could strike her captain down.

Captain Lemoine lowered himself and spun. With a smooth motion, he sliced through the English pirate's middle. The aggressor fell over, clutching his middle which was spilling onto the deck. Emily exhaled for her stomach's sake.

Her captain regained his footing, and with a hand hovering over his injured rib, he reached out and pressed her to his chest. "Are you injured?"

For the first time in several hours, she felt safe. Emily shook her head against his taut chest, tears wetting her face, and emotion caught in her throat. The captain kissed her forehead in such a fast motion Emily wasn't sure it actually happened. He turned to the rail and shouted, "Enough! Truce!"

Under the protective wing of the captain's arm, Emily noticed the bodies covering the deck were more enemy than friendly. Somehow, someway, with fewer hands than the enemy, the *Sea Lion* prevailed. To spare more lives, Emily was grateful the captain offered the other ship a chance to recover, rather than attempt to take them over.

The other captain seceded at once. "Truce!"

At once the few remaining skirmishes ended—mutual respect for their captains' orders. The foreign crew crossed back to their ship, some limping, others carrying their dead, while respectfully taking turns with the *Sea Lion*'s crew returning likewise. The enemy pirates slipped the planks back onto their side. Emily approached Fergus and checked his throat for a pulse. She felt nothing, and with a heavy heart, she lowered Fergus's eyelids.

A hand rested on her shoulder, and Emily stood to meet the captain. She wiped tears away. "What a waste. All he wanted to do was keep me safe, get me away from here." Emily gestured to the field of bodies. "And he was right to do it."

The captain brushed her chunk of sticky hair from her face. "I desire to comfort you, and I wish to tell everyone about you, about us, but I cannot. I also cannot assure you the danger is over, but I find a personal guard for you."

All this effort. All these lives. Anger spewed the words from her mouth. "What's the point of a personal guard when half the men on the ship are dead? Can we even sail back to Nassau? Is Giles, the cook alive? Why did you order them to attack? Why not just search for treasure next to them? This was all pointless! I can't believe after everything you said, you are, in fact, willing to kill and steal for money—the most selfish and depraved a man could be."

The captain recoiled as if struck by her words, and his lips parted, but when he spoke, there was an icy rage, "There shall be enough pieces of eight for us to do as we please, wherever we please it."

Emily's features twisted, and anger roared through her veins. She was shocked by Tyler's greed, and now she knew better. She should've expected it from pirates, of all people. The anger was at herself, for believing these men to be different, for not believing Fergus, who was now dead. "You know money will not get me home. Is there not a single way you could earn a living besides"—she used Fergus's descriptors—"Murdering and thieving?"

The captain's features darkened as if he'd taken offense, and she wanted to slap him. "We banded together under an agreement to seek our fortunes off the backs of wealthy merchants, who cared nothing for their employees. We were starved, refused wages, punished for minor infractions and accidents, and lived in cramped, unsanitary sleeping quarters. We live by only the code we signed on for, and we stay together until every man has earned 1,000 pieces of eight. Here at the sunken galleon, we'll collect 1,000 each, courtesy of Spain."

Emily remembered that article, but she hadn't known what it meant at the time. The history books were right—pirates murdered for money. She'd deluded herself. And whatever this attempt at something meaningful between her and the stubborn pirate captain only wasted her time. When a man was fueled by greed, how could she ever trust him?

Emily stomped away to blow off steam. "If any of the injured need me, I'll be on the orlop deck. No thanks to you." At the ladder, Boatswain Karl waited for her in desperate need of tending to his leg. She asked, "Can you climb down to get it dressed? I cannot carry you."

Karl chuckled. "I expect not."

Emily climbed down ahead of him to ready her work space. She laid out an array of ancient unsterile tools and grimaced at her patient's injuries. Karl plopped onto a barrel next to her. He pinched an eye shut to protect it from blood smearing his vision. Emily swiped it away for him, finding no gashes underneath. Must've been the other man's blood.

"That was quite the speech there, doctor." Karl grunted and used his arms to move his injured thick leg.

Emily cleaned off the gash in his thigh and threaded her needle. "This is going to sting."

The boatswain chuckled, bouncing his round middle. "No more worse than my leg, I wager."

Emily dunked her threaded needle in a small cup of rum she'd secured ahead of time and smiled. "Be careful, gambling is against the rules."

Karl laughed, and Emily made the first stitch. "Is this a normal occurrence?" she asked absently, referring to the abrupt order by the captain to invade another ship, but she feared questioning his authority directly, especially in front of witnesses.

"A cut from a cutlass? Aye, normal as can be. For a doctor, you are small and delicate of hand."

Emily darted him a look. "My appearance has nothing to do with my abilities."

"Aye." He didn't sound convinced. Emily tore the slashed fabric wider and continued stitching the gash by the poor light. Other pirates below deck made their way to the main deck, for whatever the captain wanted them to do next, she didn't care. "And you survived the fight. That's the surprising part."

"Why?" Emily squinted at him. She knew she was helpless, but that didn't mean she appreciated others pointing it out.

"Two good men protected you, one with his life. I wager the outcome would've been different had they not bothered."

Emily poked the needle through his skin rougher than necessary.

"I see how the captain looks at you. Never guessed he fancied men."

Emily's hand jerked and rather than crying out, the boatswain chuckled again. "It's not for me to know. But so long as I have my vision, I miss nothing. Curious, why do you disapprove of the captain so heartily? We take what we wish—it's our bond—and we all want riches to escape the life before the noose catches us. The captain most of all."

"I noticed the captain, more than the rest of you, takes pleasure in hunting other people's money, thank you." Her tone was sharp and condescending, but since she was covered in the blood of men and stitching one who didn't know how to keep his trap shut, she determined her attitude wouldn't get her in trouble—at the moment.

Emily quietly growled in fury as blood leaked from the deck above and dripped onto her shoulder. The air was too hot and stunk like the fetid soup she'd used to mop the merchant ship's deck. The lack of windows made her small workplace even more claustrophobic. And this jerk wasn't helping any.

Boatswain Karl laughed. "You make no sense. A pirate, like the rest of us, agreed to go on the account together, and now you changed your mind?"

Emily finished the last stitch and cleaned her needle. "I don't know what I want right now. You're done, so get out of my area and send the next survivor over."

"Be careful," Karl said, repeating her warning, only his had a serious tone to it. "The captain has his reasons for what he's doing. He deserves our respect for the time he remains."

This got Emily attention. "What do you mean 'the time he remains'? Is he sick?"

Karl stood. "That stunt you pulled with the remaining rum barrel. Know why it landed you in a heap of trouble with the quartermaster?"

"I made him look like a liar?" Emily's tone was clipped, but she was happy to listen.

"Half the crew was unsettled from the paltry prizes we'd had lately, and you noticed the stirrings of a mutiny. After we recover this prize, Captain Lemoine plans to retire from the account—woeful news for most of us, but joyous news for the dissenters. Price had been squirreling that measly rum away for the celebration. You know how strongly men feel about their rum."

Emily put away her needle. "None of that is justification for slaughtering people for their money."

Boatswain Karl shifted his weight with a grunt. "And that, good lad, is why you'll never survive as a pirate. I wish you luck in repairing injuries. You're going to need it."

He had no idea.

Chapter 23

Since Emily had declined to use whatever the strange objects in the doctor's chest were, she'd emptied her personal spool of thread stitching the crew's injuries. One man suffered a mortal wound to the chest. His mates didn't object to her offering him copious rum. Emily could do nothing but hold the man's hand while he passed.

After collecting fresh air from the main deck and vomiting over the port side rail, Emily swiped a sweaty forearm across her face and leaned against the bulwark, exhausted. A few men groaned as they lined up bodies of their fallen while others retrieved the hammocks. One by one, they wrapped the bodies in their own hammocks and sewed them closed. The quartermaster announced the name of each man as a pair of survivors lifted and discarded the body overboard. The crew fell silent until the melancholy ceremony ended. McKee, the master gunner, led the crew to inventorying the weapons and ordering their servicing. Boatswain Karl collected some men to repair lines sliced during battle.

Half a dozen ships or more, each giving the others a wide berth, had dropped anchor along the coast. One flew the Spanish flag, but it never assaulted the opportunists, not like how the captain had. Emily recognized the location and information from her reading. This must've been the infamous Plate Fleet Wreck of 1715, when a hurricane had surprised the fleet of Spanish treasure ships on their routine route from Havana to Spain. Fifty-foot waves crashed many of them into coastal rocks and swallowed others whole. Only the frigate escort who'd set off ahead of the fleet to warn away any incoming ships had escaped the storm. The sunken gold had been overwhelmed by opportunists, so the Spanish salvaged what they could, rather than waste precious time chasing off thieves.

Seven million pieces of eight were lost, hundreds of crew drowned, and the few survivors constructed camps out of the wreckage only to succumb to injuries or dehydration. But the men around her were only after the gold. To Emily, it was grave robbing. Just because this was Captain's last account before retiring didn't excuse his actions on this day.

Around thirty men had survived on the *Sea Lion*. A handful cleaned the deck of spilled blood. Giles, the cook, brought water to those remaining. Since he'd survived, they wouldn't starve, not that stale crunchy biscuits and salted pork were all that appetizing, anyway. If the waters steadied, the cook might fire up the pit, frying a portion of meat to chase away the hangry. After a battle, Emily figured all the men needed a hearty meal. Her stomach was too shaken to consider food.

The men not tasked with cleaning copied the English, using a ballast rock to sink below the surface and retrieve their own loot, since the captain failed to steal their opponent's. Pirates carried handfuls of gold and silver to a barrel secured by a few of the crew holding serviced weapons. She stared holes in the back of the captain's head and folded her arms across her chest. If Captain Lemoine had sent men for their own loot in the first place, a full quarter of their men wouldn't have died.

Why she ever thought they could work was beyond her. Some stupid fantasy where she let her research and TV shows color the reality of living among thieves and murderers. Captain Lemoine was no different from Tyler, a man who cared more about money than people, who would do anything to get it. Perhaps Tyler wouldn't have killed people, but thankfully, she'd never find out firsthand. And here she was, watching the worst depraved thing she could ever see—dead bodies dumped overboard while greedy men smiled at their twinkling precious pieces of eight, swiped from watery graves.

From a history fanatic's viewpoint, Emily wanted to see what the handmade gold and silver coins looked like brand new, but showing interest in what they were doing was against all she believed good in the world.

Emily was close enough to Florida's coast to jump into the sea and make a swim for it—sharks or not—but how long would she survive with nothing but the clothes on her back, a waterlogged cell phone, melted chocolates, and a used up sewing kit? Making a swim to the shore meant she'd starve or die of dehydration, just like the hurricane survivors. But there was something else she could do. With all hands preoccupied, Emily climbed down the ladder to the hold, left unguarded since the battle, and slipped inside. She hadn't seen Hooper. Perhaps he was one of the dead.

Emily lit a candle. The ship had restocked at Nassau, but now she didn't feel the pressure of time. She didn't care if she got caught. She pushed aside small boxes, sifted through open-top crates of green glass bottles with onion-like shapes, and shook barrels, but none of them budged. Standing and stretching under the low ceiling, Emily looked around, outstretching the candle for better light. Where would a small valuable necklace be kept safe?

The door behind her opened with a squeak of the hinges. Emily gasped from being startled, not about being caught. Regardless of the why, she'd dropped the candle. Flames licked at the fluffy crate packaging, and the man who'd caught her shouted for help. The fire grew rapidly, and men rushed in carrying buckets of sea water. They heaved water at the rapidly spreading flames.

"Fire! There be a fire in the hold! More water!" The voices carried through the floors and more footsteps thundered above. A crushing weight settled over her. Emily had already lost everything once, because of Tyler, and now she was on the verge of losing everything again. This time instead of money, it was her future hanging in the balance. Not knowing what else to do and worried her necklace was going to sink with the ship, Emily removed her sodden jerkin and swatted at the base of the flames.

Buckets splashed around her, soaking her not-so-white-anymore tunic, but the flames kept spreading. Emily swatted again and again as smoke filled the hold. Men coughed. Emily's eyes stung from the thickening haze. More buckets came, and Emily folded onto her hands and knees, spreading the seawater and patting out the flames.

"Move faster!" Emily shouted. They had to turn the tables on the fire before it reached the flash point. Not only would the firefighters all be dead from the heat, but the ship would be a total loss—leaving the survivors stranded on the coast. If she survived the flash point explosion, she'd already made too many enemies to survive the punishment. With each heave of water and whack of flames, the battle slowly shifted into the crew's favor. And with each patch of snuffed flame, more smoke billowed into the small room. Emily lifted the front of her wet shirt to breathe through, and as the heat baked them all, sweat rolled down her body.

The crew around her fought just as hard as she did. No one quit. No one fled. And finally, she heard a hiss as she patted out the last of the flames. What felt like hours was merely minutes. Smoke poured from the hold. Men waved fabric to force it out faster. The watering in her eyes turned to actual tears. Their supplies were destroyed. Likely her necklace was melted, damaged, destroyed.

Hugging her jerkin to her chest, Emily sobbed. A firm hand gripped her shoulder and led her out of the hold. "Nothing more to be done here. Come."

Emily followed on heavy feet, waving the air in front of her face, wishing for a fresh breath. She climbed up to the main deck and fell to her knees still hugging her jerkin like a teddy bear. Any chance she had of returning home was over. The entire crew was going to hate her for destroying the hold. As Price had warned, she would get no second...or third...or whatever chance. She'd lost count. How were they going to eat now?

"What happened?" Captain Lemoine shouted at his men.

Many of them looked at the deck, unwilling to meet the captain's glare.

Emily sank back on her heels, wishing to be anywhere but here, and she let the tears of remorse fall.

"Fire in the hold. Porter set fire to the hold!" The voice was unfamiliar, but Emily didn't bother to see who the accuser was. Did it even matter? She felt the captain's glare, but Emily couldn't react. Her mind was a blanket of sadness suffocating her. Never again would she see home. Never again would she see her friends, greet her coworkers, water her plant. Tyler won. He never had to repay her, since she'd be reported as a missing person soon—by someone.

She didn't know for sure who would discover her missing and care enough to report it. Maybe her boss, but not because he cared, only because she'd missed a shift and he hated wasting his time trying to find people to cover for her.

No more bills. No more pizza delivery, Netflix, hot showers...all the things Emily considered her life were now lost forever. The mourning settled upon her soul like an anchor tied to her ankles and dropped into the cold depths of the sea, slowly darkening, slowly crushing, and lungs screaming at the last flickers of life. Tears wet her face as Emily involuntarily gasped for the fresh air that wouldn't come.

She wanted a hug. The only one who'd be willing stared daggers at her.

More men rattled off their anger. No matter how hard she'd tried to fit in, one mistake ripped the trust clean away. Emily sniffled and listened to another man's accusation. "The fire 'twas an accident, but Porter was stealing, I wager."

"A thief among us!" Another called.

"There're rules against stealing from your own men, captain. He needs punishment."

Shouts of agreement poured from angry pirates' mouths.

Their assumption wouldn't change the outcome, but regardless, they were right. She was trying to steal.

"I'll handle the punishment," the captain said, and the men stood around waiting for immediate rectification.

"Back to work. Bring up the gold."

Men climbed down the side of the ship and jumped into the water with a rock in hand. The quartermaster approached the captain, and Emily stared at the deck boards, where only hours ago, blood pooled like a lagoon. "We have enough provisions to survive the trip back to Nassau. Fourteen sets of slops. Two barrels of wine, and one crate of punch. The rest is a total loss."

The rest? It was true then. Her necklace was nothing more than melted metal and—what happened to gems when they overheated?—charred or melted amethyst. Emily stared at her open palms, coated in soot and sea water, sweat and blood...and tears.

"The cooper insisted Porter caused the fire. Can you confirm?" the captain asked his quartermaster.

"Several witnesses agree. He was in the hold and started the fire. As this affects everyone, we'll hold a vote for the punishment." Price's tone was just as sharp as the first time.

The crew didn't cheer. There was no celebrating this.

Price leaned into the captain's ear and whispered. The captain nodded. Price then spoke up again for all to hear, "And it won't be lenient or disregarded this time."

A chill shivered down her soaked spine, and Emily clutched the jerkin. It was sodden, and she didn't want to put it back on.

Price marched below deck, and the remaining crew resumed salvaging the Spanish gold. The captain closed the distance. She couldn't look at him.

"I didn't steal anything," Emily blurted, staring at his leather boots. They reminded her of her own handmade boots—so similar. According to these men, she was one of them, a pirate. A thief. But worse, because she screwed up at every turn. Emily couldn't follow the rules. "The fire was an accident."

"Come with me," the captain helped her to her feet and led her into his cabin. Emily sat on the edge of his bed and remembered the last time they'd been here. Happier, more naïve, times. Still, her mind flashed back to touching the captain and kissing him feverishly. Seemed like a lifetime ago.

The captain paced the cabin, showing no signs of his aching ribs. Adrenaline must've been coursing through him.

"The quartermaster learned the crew believes you are a woman."

"What? How?" Emily blurted and stood. She touched her middle and realized her jerkin was off—to fight the fire. And underneath, her thin white tunic showed her tank top and breast shape clearly. Emily wrapped her arms across herself, hiding her chest.

"You were in the hold, and I can imagine why. Accidents happen. But you signed the articles, and the crew shall not forgive a woman on board."

There was no use in jesting about signing as Emile. "What will they do to me?" Emily asked, absently. She remembered all the favorite pirate punishments—cat-o'-nine-tails, marooning, keelhauling, duel to the death, dunking, hanging, being sold into slavery, tying to the mast for an indeterminate amount of time until delirium set in. If she could avoid keelhauling or a duel, the rest she could survive. Maybe.

"The longer I can delay them, the better off you'll be since the gold will lift their spirits. The vote is on the morrow at dawn."

Emily stood with a frown and stuffed her arms through the holes of her jerkin, ignoring the ickiness of it, and fastened the buttons. "You're the captain. Don't you have the power to do anything but decide whether to engage in battle?" She was still upset with him, but all the fight drained out of her with those tears.

"Even if the crew accepts the fire as an accident, there is no chance I can ask them to overlook a woman on board, who'd been in the hold again. Fergus and Hooper may have told a single person about their lie, and that's all it would take for them to never believe you were innocent down there."

"Yet *you* allowed me on board." Blaming the captain for her actions was immature, but a fresh sting at the injustice of it all brought back the anger.

"I didn't know you were a woman when you signed," the captain answered calmly.

"Or what? You'd have stopped me?"

The captain met her eyes, but he stood firm, strong, straight. He didn't need her any longer. "Your skills are invaluable, and I'm grateful for the time we've had."

Tears waved in her vision. "That sounds an awful lot like 'goodbye.'"

The captain walked to the cabin door and paused with a hand on the knob. He said quietly, "I may harbor many regrets in life, but I do not regret you."

Captain Lemoine left the room, and Emily fell back onto the bed. She had until morning to earn mercy from the crew.

EMILY HAD NOTHING TO offer them as a bribe. They wouldn't listen to reason, and they had every right to. She'd broken the rules the minute she signed. These men were exactly what history said they were: thieves and murderers. Emily was never, could never, hurt another person. She honestly didn't understand how Price could do his job, but that was neither here nor there.

That left thieving. Could she be like them—not just in spirit but in reality? Could she become like Tyler and Captain Lemoine? Hooper and Price? Even Giles and Karl? If she did this, Fergus would've died for nothing. All he wanted was to save her from these people, this life, and here she was, considering volunteering.

Since those men believed she was a pirate, granted an unwanted *woman* pirate, her actions to save her own life didn't matter to them. They wouldn't judge her helping to pay them in both reparations and forgiveness. But doing this would make her despicable, a real, true pirate. Whether or not she could live with it mattered not. She couldn't guarantee they'd accept her offering. But if she did nothing, they were going to kill her, anyway.

Emily sat up on the captain's bed and stuffed her red kerchief away for safekeeping. She looked at her pouch. Her things were no longer of value, but they were all she had left of the life she knew. Emily untied the pouch and set it on the bed. She stood, chin held high and left, her soul forever on the captain's bed.

Emily swallowed her stubborn pride and self-righteousness and approached the salvage crew. "Can I help?" she asked, wretchedness on her tongue.

Hyde, the night watchman who tried to rat her out to the captain, snarled at her. "No woman shall touch my gold. You be an untrustworthy bootless bugger and a thief. Go below deck and patch some wounds. Be useful while you still can."

A man next to him Emily hadn't met said with a slimy smirk, "Hyde, she can touch the gold. We'll take turns thoroughly searching her afterward." The chuckles from them both chilled her blood. "Besides, mate, if the sharks make a meal of 'er, then we don't have to waste time with a vote."

Emily peered over the edge of the rail, watching the divers going down and up. The water was about twenty feet deep, and a lot warmer and clearer than Lake Michigan waters. She could handle that. Emily inhaled deeply several times and gripped a ballast rock. She positioned herself with feet dangling over the clear blue water. The waves had settled a little, but the very bottom was obscured. She'd always said she'd rather take her chances with the sharks. Now she proved to herself she was strong enough for this.

If they killed her anyway, at least she could see firsthand what that handmade gold looked like. On that happy note, Emily launched herself headfirst into the salty sea. Having only swam in freshwater before, the Caribbean was more buoyant than she'd expected. While using the weight of the rock to help her reach the bottom, she fought to reach the bottom, legs thrashing.

Emily marveled, too briefly, at the coral reef before seeking out treasure galleon debris. Her free hand brushed at the sand, lifting a small cloud of sand and uncovering a glinting metal coin. Emily slipped it into her pocket and brushed again. Each handmade coin bore differing defects, and each had a unique stamp from its origin. They shimmered in the light—a bright, beautiful piece of history.

After finding a pocketful, she released the rock and swam up to the surface. Gasping for air, she climbed up the wooden grips and held out her pocketful of shiny pieces of eight.

Hyde accepted them with a grim set to his mouth. "This doesn't change anything."

One handful, maybe not. Emily collected another ballast rock and sank to the bottom of the sea.

Chapter 24

Handful after handful hadn't been enough to prevent the vote. Emily should've figured there was no satisfying a bunch of greedy pirates. Fergus, despite his misguided attempt to keep her safe, felt like her only ally, and now she had no one left at all. It was isolating and the feeling of dejection sank into her bones, while the cutting of tight ropes sank into her flesh. Bound to the mainmast, grimy and salty faces stared at her, and she swallowed a dry lump.

Because she wanted what was rightfully hers, she was hated. Because she tried to take it back, she would be killed. And because of her anatomy, the men wouldn't hear reason.

When Captain Donald Sinclair had her bound to his mast, she'd kissed the wood. This time, the pirates bound her facing them. The *Sea Lion* hadn't yet set a course to return to Nassau. The men continued hauling up what they could, but the divers admitted this spot was nearly cleared out. They would need to move along the coast.

Emily worked at the stinging ropes, cutting and burning her bleeding wrists. She'd take her chances swimming with the sharks to the Florida coast. Maybe the Spanish refugees would treat her better, despite the language barrier.

Price approached with a creased brow, but his hands held nothing but a clipboard. No cat for her...yet. "Emile Porter is accused of theft in the hold."

The men mumbled.

"Porter is also responsible for the fire that destroyed nearly all our belongings and supplies."

Angry grumbles and shouts came from the crowd, and Emily blinked back tears.

"Finally, Porter made a fool of us all. He is not a 'he' at all. Porter is a woman!" Now angry shouts and dirty remarks flew at her like heat-seeking missiles, and Emily learned firsthand what 'swearing like a sailor' meant. They were brutal, but thankfully, she didn't understand all of it.

"Will anyone come to *her* defense?" the quartermaster emphasized her gender pronoun as if it were a sour pill, and his tone dared anyone who spoke up.

While burying her tears, hurt and anger boiled within. How could these men, who'd treated her as one of their own, turn their backs on her the instant they learned she was born with boobs? What difference did it make? Emily searched the unkind crowd for the captain while another onslaught of slurs flew her way. Emily exhaled a shaky breath. Her fingers pulled at the restraints and so far, they wouldn't budge. If nothing else, they knew how to securely restrain a person.

No one was going to defend her, so she had to do it herself. If nothing else, her delay bought time to escape. "I am defending myself. I'm a competent doctor on this ship. I've helped patch many of your wounds, without which, you would've bled out. Some of you owe me your lives."

Quartermaster Price stepped up to her and spoke privately, "We can find a new doctor on nearly any prize we take. Seducing the captain is inexcusable, as is hiding your true nature. The number of transgressions you have accumulated in such a short time makes your presence on this vessel a greater liability than an asset, and as such, one way or another, we'll remove you."

Emily whispered back on a hiss, "Not that it's any of your business, but I never seduced the captain. I treated his wounds and saved his life. I also retrieved a hefty pail's worth of gold for you. Does that not count either?"

Technically, the captain had seduced *her*, but that was unnecessary nuance.

"We all signed the articles, and breaking them has consequences. This is not a negotiation. The vote is final. The captain has accepted his own impending punishment with dignity. You could learn a thing or two from that."

Emily's lip lifted in a silent snarl. Price was the most brash and irritating man she'd ever met, but she understood how he had power over the crew. He was logical and reasonable—for his time.

The quartermaster continued louder for everyone to hear, "One vote per man. Porter is guilty. Your decision is to choose which punishment fits her crimes: selling her into slavery or marooning."

Emily's heart sank.

"For the first option, I estimate we'd receive thirty pounds for her skills in doctoring, provided she return to her status as a man. That sum shall be split according to your share of prizes. Show of hands for the first vote: selling her into slavery."

Cheers filled her ears. Emily couldn't do the conversion in her head, but she'd wager the pail of gold she'd brought up from the bottom of the sea and gladly handed over was worth far more. Somewhere deep inside, these pirates cared about something more than money. It was the principal. The show of power.

"Second vote," Price called. "Marooning! Standard agreement states she receives a pistol with shot and powder, one day's worth of water, and one biscuit. A merciful finish to one's endless transgressions."

More cheers erupted, but Emily couldn't count the difference in hands.

While Price tallied up his count on paper, Emily said, "I gave you more than thirty pounds in gold. Despite my *transgressions*, I'm more valuable to the *Sea Lion* crew than a thirty-pound sale."

Hyde spoke up, "Keep her doctoring skills until we find the right spit of land, a perfectly bald lump of sand, clear of any shade, just waiting for the tide to take her."

"Aye, aye!" More cheers, and Emily suddenly hated them all.

The quartermaster calmed them all down. "The hands are counted. Punishment is as follows: Porter is to continue her skills while clapped in irons to prevent any new transgressions. When we reach the aforementioned spit of land, as Hyde so eloquently proposed, Porter shall be marooned."

The rattle of chain sank Emily's stomach. Hyde, a waif of a man, brought forth the iron manacles. Men moved forward and cut her ropes just as the manacles closed over her wrists. Any chance of swimming to freedom was now gone.

Hyde dragged her below deck to sit where her doctor's equipment was—along with lingering smoke haze, dried blood smears, and a light so dim her eyes struggled to see. Hyde locked her chains around the mizzen mast and walked away without a word.

Emily leaned against the mast and cried. She'd give anything to be back home. Even Tyler had never treated her so terribly. He was right to ridicule her love of pirate history. The fascination of reading about the brutal men was nothing compared to living it. Pretending to be a pirate was the stupidest hobby, the biggest waste of time. What good had it done her? She'd failed to be one convincingly, and now she was chained below deck.

If the *Sea Lion* were attacked, she'd be helplessly killed or drowned with the ship. Otherwise, soon they'd drop her off on a patch of sand that may only offer a reprieve for a few hours before the tide washed away her footing, and the weight of the manacles drowned her. Emily had no way home after the fire that she'd caused. All hope was lost, so wishing to go home wasted brain power.

If she survived this, never again would a man use and discard her. And never again would she blink at a man who put his selfish greed over another human being's life.

Emily daydreamed of how things could've been different. If she'd told Captain Sinclair her gender, would he have brought her to a city, safe and sound? What if she told the pirates upon meeting them she was a skilled woman? Would they have allowed her onboard to use her skills, knowing she wasn't a liar?

If only she hadn't sneaked into the hold, she wouldn't be chained to a mast. She just might've been in the captain's quarters on the verge of breaking other rules instead. Images of the captain's smiling face and soft lips came to mind. For a short while, she thought they could figure out something to make their relationship work, but clearly, he'd only been taking advantage of her. Now the game was over, and he'd cast her aside. Captain Lemoine didn't bother to show up for the vote. He clearly didn't care about her...like she cared about him. That made her pathetic.

Glancing at the filthy floor and imagining it was her favorite pizza place, Emily wistfully smiled at an invisible slice of fat greasy pizza. She chuckled. If only her friends could see her, they'd never believe her. Were they back home now? Had they found a more pleasant adventure? Emily was finished with adventure after this. That wanderlust was officially cured.

Wooden steps of the nearby ladder creaked as a man climbed down, and Emily swallowed her anger, ready to treat the patient who was injured through no fault of his own. But that didn't mean she had to be gentle about it.

The captain entered her infirmary.

Emily stood, the rattle and weight of metal an all-consuming reminder of her misplaced trust. "Where were you?"

His features were somber as if he regretted the course her actions had taken her. So much for the big rescue, jerk.

Captain Lemoine closed the distance and glanced around for witnesses before embracing her. Emily's bound fists pounded against his chest in feeble frustration, rattling the cold metal shackles. Emily sniffed and blinked back tears of betrayal and rage.

"I've done all I can without losing the crew. When we dock at Nassau, you'll be delivered safely ashore, never to behold the *Sea Lion* again." The captain softened his grip on her.

Emily swiped her tears. She wasn't going to drown during high tide on a spit of abandoned sandbar. Somehow the captain had renegotiated on her behalf to be 'marooned' into society, a society she'd never survive. "It doesn't matter. Without my necklace, I can't go home."

The captain brushed a lock of hair away from her eyes, his fingertips grazing gently across her cheek. He swiped away tears with tenderness. "I cannot jeopardize my standing with the crew further. Without their trust, I cannot protect you. Consider Nassau a mercy." Captain Lemoine turned away, about to climb back up to his high post.

"I don't want mercy! I want to go home!" Emily shouted, not caring who heard.

Captain Lemoine paused with a foot resting on a rung and whispered, "So do I."

Taken aback, Emily quietly watched the captain climb out of sight and swiped the remaining tears from her cheeks. Her heavy manacles clanked. She sat down heavily on her barrel of shame, remembering Boatswain Karl claiming the captain wanted to retire. Well, good for him. What did that matter to her?

An injured man, scraped by the barnacles on the hull, needed tending to, and as the pirates continued their pursuits of the gold beneath the sea, a steady stream of minor injuries trickled through her dark and dank infirmary. None of them were friendly, and not one made small talk.

Tending to them with her wrists restrained was extra difficult, but having pride in her work had long since washed away.

Chapter 25

THE PIRATES HAD TAKEN all they could while still capable of surviving the journey back to Nassau. Meanwhile, Emily had been chained to the mizzenmast on the orlop deck until the injuries diminished. Then she'd been sitting with Giles, peeling potatoes he'd been preparing in the kitchen during the fire. Her wrists ached with the scratchy cold metal, her arms ached with the weight, and her hands were sliced, trying to use a knife to peel with a rocking ship underfoot. But finally, they'd returned to port, and she'd been allowed on the main deck. The fresh air and sunlight were a welcome reprieve from the ship's humid and dank belly that still lingered with the scent of burned wood.

With a scowl, Hyde released the shackles at her wrists. Instantly her arms sagged with relief, and she rubbed her aching shoulders.

"Should've been desolate. You don't deserve this, but Price said he'd made a deal in the crew's best interest." Hyde spat on the deck by her feet. "Fancy that."

Emily didn't respond. Nothing she could say would change anyone's mind. Sailors worked the pulleys to set up the longboat for her. Holding her chin high, Emily climbed aboard when authorized to do so, and men filled the seats around her. A pair lowered them to the water's surface.

The captain wasn't one of them, and once again his inaction confused her. His kisses and words said he cared, and the deal he'd made with Price to exchange a spit of land for Nassau said he cared. But his lack of appearance said otherwise.

The pirates rowed, delivering her to an outstretched dock in Nassau. She stood on wobbly sea legs and shuffled to the rocking boat's edge, sloppily climbing up and out. Not one of them said a word to her, nor assisted, and they tied the boat to the pilings and climbed out, leaving her to purchase new supplies with her ill-gotten gold. But their spirits weren't high for the brothel as she'd expected.

"What about a gun with shot, water and a biscuit? That was part of the terms." Emily had no money. She at least wanted food and water.

One of the pirates leaned close while passing her. "Terms of your punishment changed, or haven't you noticed?"

Shielding the sun from her eyes, she searched the ship's rail, seeking the captain, but he wasn't there. None of the men watched her departure, except two who were simply awaiting the longboat's return.

Emily faced Nassau, the pirate haven filled with miscreants and less than savory rules. She walked down the dock, uncertain where her feet carried her. With no chance of returning home, no food or money, Emily had only one choice: survive in the primitive pirate world. She'd left her pouch on the captain's bed. He hadn't returned it. Emily needed a job.

The city bustled with activity. Men carried lumber on their shoulders, the blacksmith's hammer fell with an ear-piercing ping, and a group of women strolled by, socializing. Strolling down the sand and stone path between tightly packed buildings, she narrowly avoided colliding with a pack of chickens and a few confused goats. She smiled at the goats, but sadness lingered. Her mother would've wanted to pet them as she had, and now Emily was never going to visit her mother's grave again. She couldn't think like that. Emily had to survive.

Emily stopped at The Golden Macaw to find a familiar face. Inside the bar-restaurant-motel, Emily sought out the woman in charge. The voluptuous woman with her curly updo—silver wig of the times, no doubt—was behind the counter, checking in a guest. Emily waited in line behind him, and when Marta was free, Emily stepped up.

"Hello!" Marta said with a friendly and bright tone, and suddenly whatever jealousy she'd felt toward the older woman was gone. "How are you, dear? Where's the captain?"

Ignoring that disappointing reminder, Emily said, "I'm looking for a job. Do you have anything available?"

Marta gave her the once over assessment and frowned. "Not like that, I don't. Come with me, deary."

"Wait," Emily said softly. "Did you know I was a woman?"

Marta smiled deviously and winked.

Emily shook her head with a smile, happy to know the events of the *Sea Lion* would not be repeated. Willing to get out of her salt-ridden and damaged handmade clothes, Emily eagerly followed the older woman around the desk. She handed her a folded stack of clothes, and Emily assumed they were the previous worker's uniform.

"What exactly do you have available?" Emily's open mind only went so far.

"A housekeeper. You'll clean rooms after they become vacant and serve the guests in the lounge."

"Is that all?"

The old woman cocked her head. "Is there something else you had in mind?"

"Nope, no." Emily shut that down. "This is great, thank you."

"When you make yourself presentable, come back for your first assignment." She turned to leave as if that was all the instruction a woman from three hundred years into the future needed.

"Where do I stay?" Emily called to her back. "I'm between homes at the moment."

She turned and smiled kindly. "Second floor just above the desk here. All my ladies who have the need, sleep there. I'm sure Daphne can make you a cot." With that, Marta left to attend her own duties, whatever they were.

In the homeless women's room, Emily changed her clothes and cringed in the mirror. Dresses so weren't her thing. Authentic, antique gowns of the eighteenth century were definitely not her thing. If they made her wear a powdered wig over her blonde hair, she'd be out the door and asking the blacksmith if he needed an apprentice.

At least she could wear pants.

A woman swooshed through the doorway on a mission, collecting linens from a cabinet. This was the staff quarters and stock room, it appeared. Her dark hair was pinned in soft waves over her shoulders, and she wore a layered dress with structure to it. The woman dropped a stack of bedding on a bare cot, startling Emily, and said, "This is yours whenever you need it. Ready to come along now?"

Lines in her face and a ruggedness showed years of labor. Emily hadn't moved, so the woman stepped forward. "I'm Daphne. You are?"

"Emily." It felt great to tell someone her real name.

Daphne kept her face impassive as Emily would've expected for someone who routinely trained new housekeepers. "Pay is not free. Follow me." Her curt turn was rude, whether she was busy or not.

Emily frowned at her back but followed. Daphne handed her a stack of clean linens from a hall closet and led her into the room next door. Emily pulled up short and covered her eyes against the naked man, who decided the best article of clothing to put on first was a shirt.

"Don't be shy," Daphne told her. "Good afternoon, Walter. Sleep well today?" Emily's mentor stripped the bed in a quick fashion while Walter smiled at Emily.

"Who's the new girl?" he asked.

"Be nice," she said without pausing in her work. "Emily, take these."

Emily rushed to the woman's side and accepted the stack of dirty linens. She fought the urge to grimace at the smell.

"Emily," he repeated. "Where you from?"

What a loaded question. Emily chose the easiest answer. "The *Sea Lion*."

The switch of the man's face told her that was the wrong answer. "Captain Lemoine's crew? How did a *woman* get aboard a pirate crew?"

With a fake smile, she answered pleasantly, "The same way a man does."

Walter laughed. "I understand now. How is Lemoine these days?"

"Can you put on pants or something?" Emily glanced aside, frustrated the man was so uncaring about his privacy. For some stupid reason, Emily felt uncomfortable around a naked man who wasn't the captain.

"Pants?" he asked, genuinely confused.

"Breeches," she clarified. "Cover up, please."

Daphne flipped fresh sheets onto the bed and asked her with narrowed eyes, "You were a pirate?"

Before Emily could answer, Walter said, "It's a shame I missed that."

Emily picked up on that detail. Squishing the sheets into a smaller, less obnoxious ball, she said, "You were on Captain Lemoine's crew?"

Walter tied his tunic closed at the throat and reached for his breeches. "For a time."

"What happened?" Curiosity overtook her sense of propriety.

"Captain Lemoine won the vote over me, so I dropped the account at the next port. Eventually I found my way back here. Too risky to be gallivanting anywhere else. What's your story?"

Emily gave him the watered-down version, like he said, too risky. "Captain Lemoine rescued me from a merchant ship. I joined until I was no longer wanted."

"Because you're a woman?" he finished.

"They didn't know for the longest time, but yes," she bit out.

Walter's sly smile irritated her. He stuffed his legs into his breeches while Daphne handled the dirty bathwater. "And that's not the only reason I wager, is it?"

Emily hadn't asked about the pay, but it better be worth tolerating the guests' nosiness. "That's none of your business."

He laughed. "Ol' Lemoine's been after a woman for far too long. Surprises me none he clings to the first one he meets. And that poor sap won the vote over me? I was a better strategist than he, but the crew ate up his tales of a sunken treasure fleet. I thought it hogwash. Well…" Walter tied his breeches, and Emily glanced at Daphne, who surprisingly wasn't giving her the stink-eye for socializing instead of working.

Walter's tale meant they crew had tried to dethrone Captain Lemoine just prior to this account. She wondered if many of them didn't believe the tale. They likely regretted that now.

"I'm feeling fortunate you joined The Golden Macaw. I expect to see plenty of you." Walter's tone suggested he intended to figure out why the captain wanted her, but Emily wasn't so sure the captain did. Otherwise, why did he let her go?

Emily said the only dismissive thing that came to her, "I hope your stay at The Golden Macaw is pleasant."

Walter's chuckle annoyed her, so when Daphne gestured for her to follow her out of the room, Emily eagerly kept on her toes. On the balcony connecting the second-floor rooms, Emily asked, "Are all the guests like that?"

"Like Walter? A few. You adjust or quit like the others. It's best not to respond in a personal way. Put the soiled linens in this hatch here, and we'll make our way to the next room."

Emily shoved the stinky load into the laundry chute and closed the small hatch. She followed her mentor until her eye caught on the table below, where she'd spent a marvelous lunch with the captain dining on turtle and fruit. He'd seemed so genuine, and she'd thought there was a mutual attraction between them, but as Walter insinuated, she was likely the result of a lack of options. Daphne handed her another stack of clean linens while Emily pushed away the crushing thoughts.

She followed Daphne into the next room, currently empty but clearly being used, and she helped her strip the bed this time.

"How long have you been here?" Emily asked her.

"Since I was a young girl."

At least that was job security. Emily couldn't picture herself entertaining naked men and cleaning their rooms forever, but money was money.

Daphne must've seen a look on her face she didn't intend. The brunette added, "It's not so bad as that. Regular customers, regular pay, and a good boss can mean the difference between a comfortable life and one of struggle. I must admit, a woman pirate is intriguing. How did you become a pirate? I mean, what were you before?"

Emily lifted the corner of the mattress and helped Daphne fold and tuck the sheets underneath, setting it down smooth, as if they were a well-oiled machine.

"A merchant captain stole my necklace, my only way home, and before being punished, the pirate captain of the *Sea Lion* rescued me, but he took it for his crew. I was a fan of pirates, from what I'd read, and I'd never met one before that day. So I joined up to get it back."

"Did you?" Daphne asked, eyes wide, captivated by her tale.

"I'm here, aren't I?"

Daphne's face scrunched. "Those scoundrels—the lot of them!—always stealing from others and never bothering to consider the damage they inflict. If those thieves' ill-gotten coin didn't keep these doors open, I'd spit on them all."

Emily chuckled and an urge to justify the captain's actions came to her lips. "They aren't all bad. Just trying to make their living like any other."

"I'm surprised you defend them after they stole from you and turned your life on its head."

Emily made a noise of acknowledgment. The woman was right. But she couldn't get the captain out of her head.

26

Chapter 26

WEEKS TICKED BY AND Emily fell into a dreary routine of fending off frustrating comments by men while cleaning up after them. Oh, how she missed the modern world!—wash machines, dishwashers, hot showers, and most of all, the ability for a woman to put a man in his place without getting slapped.

She also missed something else. Emily brushed away tears. The loneliness was so painful. She had no one to talk to. No one who knew her or understood.

Captain Lemoine and his sweet lips never left her mind. She stewed over him all day long, every day. The longer they were apart, the worse the pain in her chest festered, as if she'd developed an infection of the heart. But Walter's words still polluted her mind. When the captain first showed he was into her, he'd believed Emily was a man, so Walter was wrong. Captain Lemoine didn't cling to the first woman he'd met, because Emily wasn't a woman at the time. The unbearable loss, worse than any she'd ever experienced before, proved Emily loved Captain Lemoine, but she was a fool for it. She allowed herself to love again, and she'd been abandoned...again.

While squirreling away her extra wages to find a home of her own, Emily had scavenged spare parts to build a sanctuary for her to visit—a small hut away from the city. She couldn't eat, sleep, and work at the same place every day for her own mental health.

Right on the edge of the beach, just under the palms, not a sound carried but the gulls cawing and waves gently lapping. A gentle breeze picked up, whisking the palm fronds together in a dance. She'd chosen this spot for the panoramic view of the coast. Emily was stuck here, so she had to find something about it to enjoy, and that was watching the comings and goings of ships at port, their broad sails, and cheers of teamwork.

Setting down a bartered hammer from the blacksmith, Emily brushed away tears from her lids, using her dirty handmade tunic sleeve. Exhausted and calloused, Emily lowered herself on a barrel she'd converted to a chair and drank from her canteen. She scanned the horizon, looking at the different shapes of sails. She told herself it was entirely out of fascination and curiosity, but every time a set flickered in the distance, her heart thumped wildly. So far, her captain's ship hadn't returned.

The withered old vendor had told her the amethyst granted true desires and protected against bad humors. Emily had told the old lady she wished to see tall ships, that was it. And, she supposed, that wish had been granted. But something was missing.

This life of back-breaking labor, bare essentials, filth, and the risk of dying every five minutes ate at her. In her previous life, she'd organized merchandise and entered override codes at the checkouts. Although not mentally stimulating, it was so much easier than this. She'd do her job, go home, and have a life. Since getting tossed off the

Sea Lion, all Emily experienced was work, work, work, and when she was too tired to lift a hand, it was work some more or starve. If this didn't count as bad humors, Emily didn't know what did.

This wasn't what she wanted. This wasn't a life. She missed her friends. She missed her home, but mostly she missed... Emily sighed softly and gazed at the sea.

EMILY PORTER HATED HIM, but Captain Lemoine couldn't live with himself if he couldn't repair the hurt he'd caused. For weeks, he'd pictured Emily's beautiful face and thought about what to say to fill the chasm between them. And now he'd journeyed back to her, and in silence, he gazed upon her as if in a new light. All alone in this little corner of the island, living in less than what he'd considered a shack. Back in poverty once again. He was right in what he'd done, and he needed her to see his side.

Mostly, Captain Lemoine hoped Emily would grant him permission to explain.

Emily sucked in a breath and glanced at the pouch in his hand. She stood at once. Emily had left it on his bed, and he didn't know if it was a thoughtless gesture or if it meant something. He hoped it meant something. When her beautiful hazel eyes landed on his face, his chest squeezed. He thought he did everything right to create a balance between keeping the crew satisfied and keeping Emily safe.

But clearly it hadn't been good enough.

She slowly stood and looked at his feet sinking in the soft, uneven sand. "How long have you been here?"

"Not long enough." Captain Lemoine moved forward, closer, and his heart pounded in his chest. He should've been here much sooner, but he couldn't. He couldn't face her with nothing to offer.

Emily's hands trembled, and she fidgeted to hide it. Her gaze traveled his body as he slowly approached, watching his gait. "Your rib must've healed well."

"I found this. I believe it belongs to you," he said, ignoring her comment and handing over the pouch with the strange device inside.

She accepted it, but didn't look in it. "Thank you."

He paused, waiting for her to send him away while clinging to that last shred of hope he'd carried as if it were the most valuable treasure in the world.

Emily set the pouch on a chair and waited.

Captain Lemoine wouldn't waste his limited time now. "I owe you an explanation. After promises had been broken so many times in your past, they are meaningless to you, but we'd made a deal, and I don't break my promises."

Emily's head tilted, blonde hair fluttering in front of her face.

"I never returned your necklace as we agreed, but I had a reason for it." The captain paused, letting his words sink in. "I didn't return it, not because the crew was owed a share of its value. Not because it had been destroyed in the fire. I toed around returning it, because I couldn't allow you to leave."

Emily squinted, confused. "You wanted me to be a prisoner?"

The captain gestured for her to sit.

Emily balanced herself on the chair, and it sank softly into the sand. Regardless if there had been another chair, Lemoine kneeled by her feet. "As you know, I had been losing the crew. My heart wasn't in the hunt any longer." He softly chuckled. "It was never in the hunt. I only yearned for the opportunity to score the one prize that would allow me to leave the account for good. Do you know what I want?"

"I would've guessed money," Emily said, "But now I assume that's not why you're here."

Well, that was not what he wanted to hear, but he had to continue, anyway. This was his one and only chance, even if he could see the sharp crags ahead about to obliterate his ship. "I am a farmer at heart, a plantation worker, but I gave it up to find the money to be worthy of the woman I loved. I became a merchant sailor to earn the money she needed, but I quickly learned that wouldn't get me there, so when the account had been explained to me, I leaped. I've been seeking that money ever since."

"I remember the story," she said dryly.

He continued, "After a few years passed, my memories of her faded, but my goal didn't change, only my reasons. I planned to buy that plantation. Not out of spite, but for the principal of it. My family still worked there, and I wanted to free them. Unfortunately, much had changed in the five and twenty years I've sailed these seas. My family had passed on or moved away onto new things."

Emily blinked, listening intently. Captain Lemoine wanted to cup her hands in his, but he waited.

"But then I met you, and I knew what I wanted right away. And when I learned you worked your whole life to fight poverty, only for your lover to steal that life from you, I vowed to do whatever necessary to return to you the money you'd lost."

Emily's face twisted with anger. "He cheated me of my life's savings by being a manipulative asshole. I hate selfish greedy bastards like him. I excused your desire for the Spanish gold, because it was a recovery mission, but the minute you chose to attack a ship full of men only trying to do the same, you lost my respect."

The captain lowered his eyes. He'd suspected she didn't understand. "What do you think would've happened had we collected barrels of gold ourselves?"

"Pirates near pirates and ships filled with treasure...?" Emily said with an edge to her voice. The anger still rumbled beneath her surface. "They would've attacked the *Sea Lion.* Exactly what you did first."

"Against an inevitability, I ordered the attack first, while we were rested and fit to increase our odds of success. But I can see how my actions disgusted you, and there's nothing more for me to say to convince you otherwise." Captain Lemoine finished pouring his heart to her. He said everything he could to convince her otherwise, but he failed. His heart squeezed in his chest, cutting off his ability to breathe. He stood to his full height and looked down at her. This was goodbye—the real and final one. He'd never see her again.

Captain Lemoine opened his palm and held it out to her. "You'll be wanting this."

Sunlight reflected off the amethyst stone on a copper chain. Emily's eyes widened in disbelief and a smile brightened her face. He'd hoped to see that face on her when he appeared, but it was not to be so. She scooped it up and marveled at it.

Captain Lemoine couldn't watch. He didn't want to see the magic that brought her to him, and he certainly didn't want to see it whisk her away to foreign, terrifying lands. With an ache still permeating his ribs and thigh, he turned and headed down the beach. Beneath the shadows of his cocked hat, he brushed away tears.

A LIGHTNESS, AN EXCITEMENT filled her for the first time in weeks. The captain had given back what mattered most to her in the world—her life, her freedom, and her right to choose. Somewhere deep inside those pirates, they cared about something more than money. Well, most of them.

Emily looked up, but the captain had made his way down the beach.

Her fingers turned the gem, failing to believe she really had it. She could go home to everything and everyone she missed. No more laundering dirty men's bedding and smiling at their rude comments. No more struggling to find food and bartering for tools, wondering if any at moment if someone wanted something more from her than she was willing to give.

The captain sank further into the distance, and the lightness in her chest dissipated, leaving behind a hollow ache. There was something she needed answered, regardless of her choice.

"Wait!" Emily shouted, and he stopped, but he didn't turn around.

Emily closed the distance, beat up leather boots sinking into the soft sand as she fought to get closer, but she wasn't willing to give up yet. Emily asked to his back, "The crew already had their gold. Why didn't you leave the ship with me?"

The captain turned around, eyes red. "You were to be marooned on a spit of land, yet you were brought here."

Emily remember the mysterious punishment he'd accepted.

"I gave them my entire share of the gold to spare your life." His gaze locked on hers as if pleading for understanding, but she didn't.

If his reasons for needing the gold had all been lost, she didn't understand, if he cared, why he didn't join her? "We could've had a life together. Why did you leave me?"

"I stayed with the crew and returned to the Florida coast."

Emily frowned. "For more money?"

"I wanted to buy that plantation for you, Emily, a life of luxury you deserved but lost."

Emily stared. The generosity was so foreign, so unnecessary. She'd never felt more respected in her life. "I didn't need money, Captain."

Her captain smiled, but still the sadness lingered. "I'm retired. Call me Eric."

Emily opened her hand with the necklace and bounced it in her palm. "There's something I need to tell you."

Eric Lemoine simply waited, a surprisingly patient man. The breeze tousled the hair fastened at the nape of his neck, and the brim of his hat fluttered. But his dark, red-rimmed eyes were locked on hers.

"I put on my homemade pirate costume for the Tall Ships festival, intending to explore history and have fun with my friends. While I was there, a woman sold me this necklace. She'd claimed it granted true desires and protected against bad humors. I've struggled to understand what she meant, but I know now. You were my protection. You are my true desire. She brought me to you. I may not have my life's savings, but I'll take having my life saved instead. I love you, Eric."

The man she loved pulled her into a tight embrace, hands pressing her as if afraid she'd disappear. Emily's lips found his. It was not the slow kiss of exploration. It was the deep, quick shifting need of desperation, of love almost lost but found, and of freedom. She clasped her hands behind his neck while molding to his body. This was a man who trusted her, whom she trusted, and who was the best thing to happen to her. The warmth of protection in his embrace felt like a fuzzy blanket and a cup of hot chocolate on a cold, snowy morning. Emily felt as if they were one; she was finally whole.

A seagull cawed overhead, and waves lapped near their feet.

Emily withdrew from his embrace and stepped back with a smile. "You are my home." She wound up her arm and heaved the necklace into the water. With a small splash, it sank into the depths, never to be found again. Not that she'd ever be tempted.

"You care not to sell it?" Eric asked, puzzled.

Emily smiled and shook her head. "I wouldn't want to curse anyone with a trip to the future. It's not all that great, trust me."

"You must tell me about it someday." Eric's brilliant smile was contagious, and they held hands as they walked along the beach back to her hut. "This is your home?"

She scratched her head. "My best effort. It's not much, but it's an escape from The Golden Macaw."

"Collect your things, we're going home."

Excited, Emily ducked inside, picked up a rough bag, and filled it with her newfound tools and other worthy purchases, but the hut and her chair were left to wither away on their own. Emily slung the bag over her shoulder and ducked back out. Eric insisted on carrying it for her, so she allowed it, happy to hang onto his arm while they walked along the coast back to town.

"Where's home?" she asked.

"You'll see." He winked at her, and Emily was excited to begin the next chapter of her adventure.

27

Chapter 27

Emily had imagined something like a cabin, in all honesty. But Eric Lemoine had twisted his words just a little. He hadn't *planned* to buy the plantation. He bought it. Eric had sent word to his remaining family members to return as owners for a life of comfort. Eric's younger brother returned at once and stepped up to manage the fields. Their reunion was testy for a while until the retired captain explained why he'd left.

Emily sipped wine from a silver cup while Eric finished his breakfast at the table. This was a level of luxury that made her uncomfortable, but unlike the shack by the beach, she could get used to hand-carved furniture and real silverware. Underfoot were hand-woven rugs—not that machine-made were an option yet—and a square footage that would scare anyone with a vacuum cleaner and a steam mop. The estate had its own cleaning crew. Emily didn't know what to do with her own staff. But since she had plenty of experience being bossed around at her retail job, she figured she could model some of those skills, although kinder.

Eric Lemoine rose from the table and dropped his embroidered napkin on the surface. At the sound of his chair scraping on the wood floor, a woman appeared. "What can I do for you, sir?" she asked politely.

"Give us a tune, Letty." Eric circled around to her, in a dashing outfit like English noblemen wore, and he held out a hand, inviting her to stand. Emily smiled and accepted. Eric had a woman with taste choose a wardrobe for her, and since the clothing fit her, and she had help explaining how and why the layers were worn, she started to like it. Her shirting was gold and the top bronze. Her corset was sage green with little gold and bronze florets. Her blonde hair had been curled and pinned back with a lock dangling behind an ear. She honestly felt like a princess.

Letty sat at the harpsichord in the corner of the room, and with music sheets in view, she began playing a song.

Emily's dress rustled as he moved them into an open space. At one of the patio doors overlooking the seaside front yard, a darkening cloud system at the horizon announced its approach with thunderous claps, carrying promises of a refreshing rain.

"Dance with me," Eric whispered, offering his hand formally.

Emily smiled at the unnecessary gesture, and he captured her in his embrace, turning her around the room in timing with the notes. He was a great lead, since Emily didn't know the steps, but she never fumbled once. After a quick spin, he dipped her and kissed her. "Marry me, Emily Porter."

"I would love to, Eric. On one condition."

Eric's brows lifted. "Name whatever your heart desires."

"Kiss me again," Emily said, biting back a playful grin.

"As the lady wishes." Eric's lips met hers once more. Emily wrapped her arms around his neck and held on for the throbbing heat accumulating down low. As if he were thinking the same thing, he scooped her up into his arms, ready to take her to bed. Bells clanged offshore, catching his attention. Eric gazed out at sea.

"Do you miss it?" she whispered into his ear.

His soft, dark eyes returned her gaze. "She calls to me, but the greatest prize I could ever imagine is standing before me now. I have no reason to answer it. Come to bed with me and we shall be wed at the earliest opportunity."

Her fiancé carried her to their bedroom. He set her on her feet and gazed into her eyes with a burning desire she'd never seen before. His fingers slipped along her jaw as he moved behind her and untied the corset, nimbly freeing the constrictive material from her body and tossing it aside. He untied the gown and freed the petticoat from her hips. Emily stepped out of them. The painstaking process was sensual. The anticipating building.

When Eric returned to her front, she took the opportunity to remove his coat and slide off his tunic, a silent, sexy movement. Her palms pressed against his chest and slid along the fine dusting of dark hair. His nipples hardened at her touch.

Eric groaned softly. He reached her for shift and slipped it up over her head. Emily went for his breeches, now tightened in the front, and she untied them, hands trembling with desire. The fabric fell to the floor, and Eric stepped free of it. His drawers were tented with his arousal. He picked her up and settled her on the bed, and as he covered her body with his, Eric's mouth found hers. Kisses moved along her mouth and throat.

Breaths came in short bursts.

His mouth moved along her body, licking and teasing each nipple, hands cupping her breasts. The muscles on his back flickered with his movements. The throbbing continued to grow, and she wanted him inside her. Eric's kisses moved along her belly, down below. He sucked at her clit and Emily arched back and moaned. His fingers found her opening while his tongue lapped at her clit. Eric found a rhythm, and he kept a slowly growing pace. Heat surged, collecting where he worked at her, urging her release, refusing to give up until he'd won.

The necklace had magic, but Eric did, too.

Emily arched again and fisted his hair in her hands, holding his face in position.

Eric didn't relent his pace. She admired his rigorous stamina. Her breaths became hitched, and finally, she climaxed.

Eric slowed while she rode the waves, and when she giggled at the tickles and pushed at him, he stopped, resting his chin on her belly and grinning. He wiped his face on the bedding and loomed over her, cock stiff and ready for use.

Emily gripped it in her palm and, for a flash, she remembered one of her favorite movies, modified for the moment, of course. Eric didn't have paper and pencil in hand. "Fuck me like one of your French girls."

Eric's brows lifted, and a stream of French came from his mouth. "*Comme vous le souhaitez, madame.*"

Emily groaned. She didn't understand what he'd said, but the sexy accent and the words made her wet all over again. Eric positioned himself, and Emily relented her grip. He moved inside her, slowly and carefully, and he leaned down. Eric wrapped his arms up under hers, and when he'd glided all the way inside, he groaned. Emily arched her back and closed her eyes.

Then he moved. Slowly at first, and quickly gaining speed. Emily wrapped her legs around him and kept the rhythm. She kissed his neck. Her fiancé lowered himself to kiss her mouth through the panting and the thrusts. Sweat beaded on his forehead. "Is this how you imagined it?" he whispered against her mouth.

Emily smiled through her panting. He was far more generous than she'd ever imagined. "It's better."

Eric groaned and stilled as he came. He lowered himself to her chest, and they rested, breathing, stroking each other's hair in a comfortable silence. She had so many more ways to explore his body, and now she had all the time in the world to do it.

Eric Lemoine was her home.

28

Epilogue

THE SHIP GROANED UNDER the swelling of the waves while they anchored at Nassau. Bright sun burned the leathery skin of all hands on board. Lemoine had been a great strategist, but the sea was never in his heart. He'd only ever wanted to collect his prize and escape back to the land, and now he and Emily had what they wanted. She was a strong woman, quick, formidable, determined. Price admired that about her, and many times when the situation aboard had been complicated, he'd regretted having to mete out punishments. Now, Quartermaster Price had a difficult task ahead of him. He had to lead an election for a new captain, and he had no idea who could fill those shoes.

"We vote!" Quartermaster Price shouted to all the new sailors crowding around him. After returning to Nassau for Lemoine to disembark for the last time, Price needed to refill their ranks. When news of their successful haul of the Spanish gold spread, Price had to beat beggars off with a stick. Now fully manned with sailors eager for their own riches, all they needed was to assign duties before heading off. These men weren't all green, and a few trusted associates remained—Cantu, Boatswain Karl Dillon, Giles, their amazing cook, McKee the master gunner, and Hodgens, the capable helmsman.

"We must choose the next captain." Heads turned and whispered to each other, and Price gave them a minute. He'd warned them ahead of time, so they could decide among themselves who to nominate. "Do we have nominees?"

Sailor Noah Riley stepped forward. "I nominate you, Henry Price."

Cheers deafened him, and Price grinned with the honor. When the noise settled, he said, "I'm the quartermaster. I do not wish to be captain." Quartermaster Price knew his strengths were in organizing the ship and keeping men on task. He wasn't the most accomplished in battle; however, he'd survived many throughout his forty years of age.

"In this, you are the best," Noah Riley argued. "And I nominate Boatswain Karl Dillon to step up as quartermaster."

With this, Karl's smile spread across his face, but he shook his head. "No, no! I'm no quartermaster, ya bumbling fools. If left up to me, we'd all stay in Nassau drinking rum and buried in women! I nominate Henry Price as captain and Noah Riley as quartermaster."

More cheers echoed around them. A voice of a crewman hanging in the rigging shouted down, "Price and Riley! Together, we shall capture the world!"

The crew chanted Price's name as successor, and he puffed up his chest in a show of acceptance. If he turned them down, he'd lose their respect, so he had no choice now. "It's settled. I'll be your captain, and Riley—you are the quartermaster." The men cheered again. "Weigh anchor while I plot our course. Be prepared for great success at sea!"

The men rushed to their stations, eager to hunt down their first prize. Price watched them.

Captain Henry Price.

Captain.

He never would've seen this coming. He hoped to be half as successful as his predecessor. And he knew exactly where he needed to go. Collecting Spain's gold wasn't enough vengeance for him. And just maybe, Price would be lucky enough to walk away with his skull intact and a bold woman on his arm.

A man could only dream.

Dear Reader,

Dive into Angela Foxe and Captain Price's story in Pirate's Treasure (Pirates in Time Book 2)!

As an indie author, I'm thrilled you decided to share your time with me, exploring the crazy worlds residing in my head and keeping me up at night. Your reviews are very important to me, so if you enjoyed this book, please consider leaving some stars for Emily Porter and Captain Lemoine's story, Pirate's Prize (Pirates in Time Book 1).

If you found any typos or errors, I blame my cat. Rat her out at: support@stephanieflynn.com.

Thank you for your support!

Also By Stephanie Flynn

Find my catalog at StephanieFlynn.com

Immortal Protector series

0.5 Vampire's Distraction

1 Vampire's Deception

2 Vampire's Secret

3 Vampire's Promise

3.5 Elf Bound

4 Vampire's Demand

Immortal Protector Side Tales

Deer Holiday

Love Claws

Depths of the Heart

Matchmaker in Time series

0.5 Minutes to Live

1 Seconds to Act
2 Hours to Arrive
3 Days to Hide
4 Years to Savor

Pirates in Time series
1 Pirate's Prize
2 Pirate's Treasure
3 Pirate's Plunder

Time Travel Romance Shorts
Fateful Time
One Crazy Time

If you like your urban fantasy without the romance, too, check out Stephanie Flynn's other name, Marie Flynn!

About Stephanie Flynn

Stephanie Flynn writes action-packed paranormal romance filled with adventure, suspense, and danger. She lives in Michigan, USA, with her husband and kids, and she spends her writing time surrounded by a herd of normal cats who bat everything off her desk, including her coffee. Check out her website for more books: StephanieFlynn.com